BLACK MINGO

Nell Glasser Smith

Contributors

Ann Glasser Milligan and
Julie Glasser Harrison

ISBN 979-8-89243-827-8 (paperback)
ISBN 979-8-89243-828-5 (hardcover)
ISBN 979-8-89243-829-2 (digital)

Copyright © 2024 by Nell Glasser Smith

All rights reserved. No part of this publication may be reproduced, distributed, or transmitted in any form or by any means, including photocopying, recording, or other electronic or mechanical methods without the prior written permission of the publisher. For permission requests, solicit the publisher via the address below.

Christian Faith Publishing
832 Park Avenue
Meadville, PA 16335
www.christianfaithpublishing.com

This is a work of fiction. Unless otherwise indicated, all the names, characters, businesses, places, events and incidents in this book are either the product of the author's imagination or used in a fictitious manner. Any resemblance to actual persons, living or dead, or actual events is purely coincidental.

Printed in the United States of America

Forever in my heart, I dedicate my first book to my parents, Howard and Jean Glasser, for their stories would have been left untold as if they never had happened.

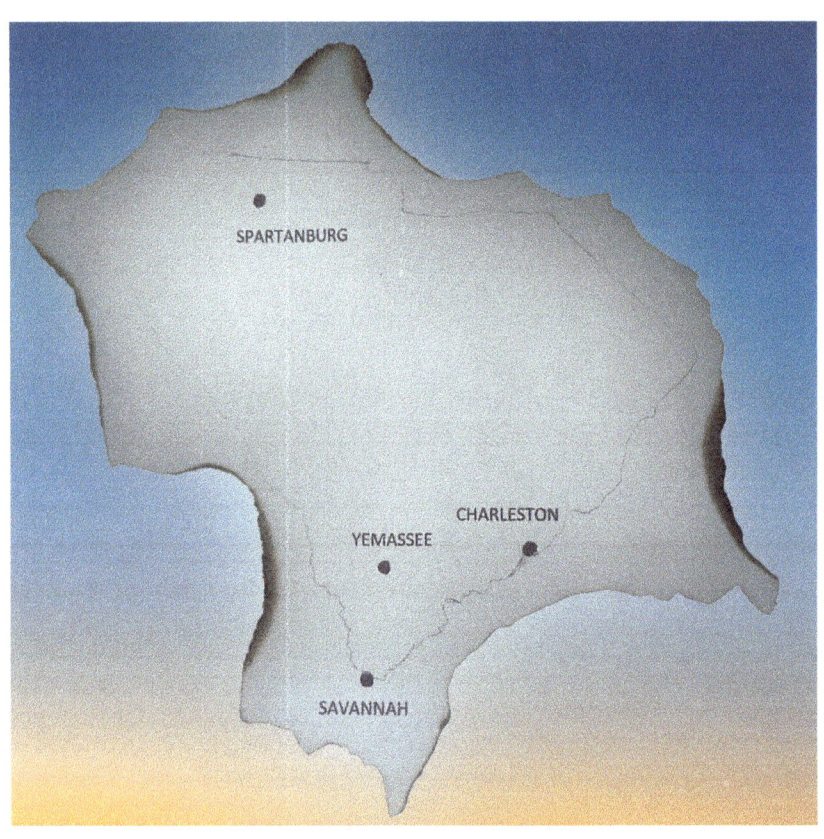

The Four Main Towns in Black Mingo

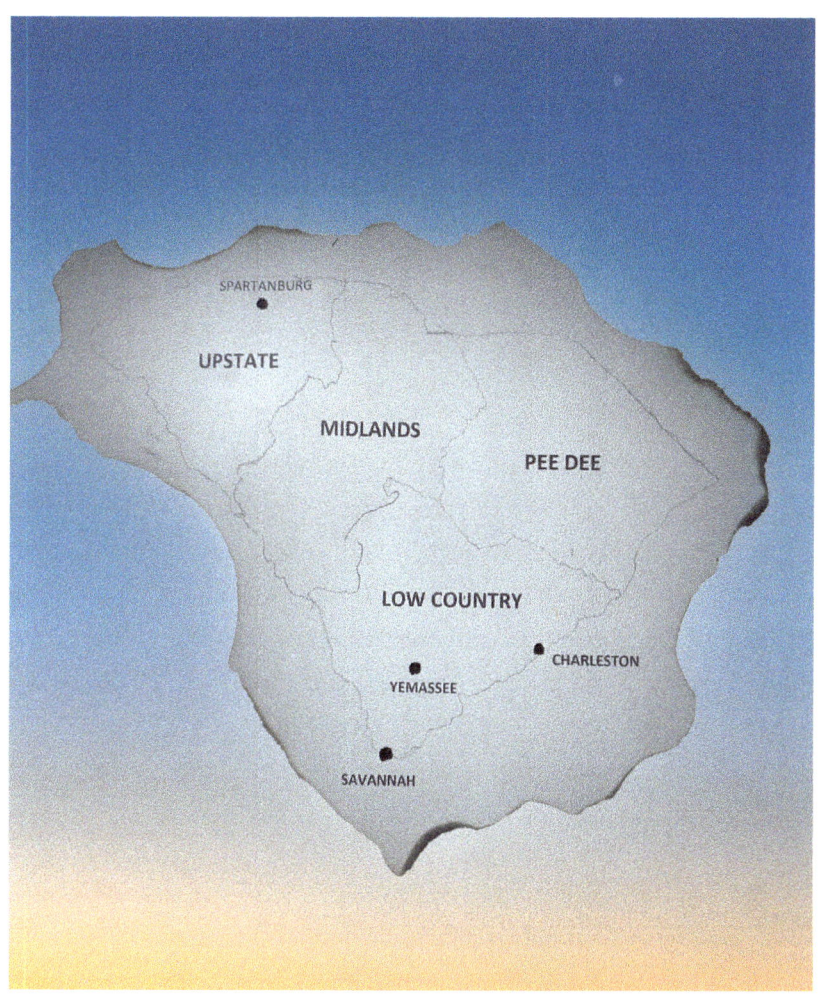

The Four Regions of South Carolina

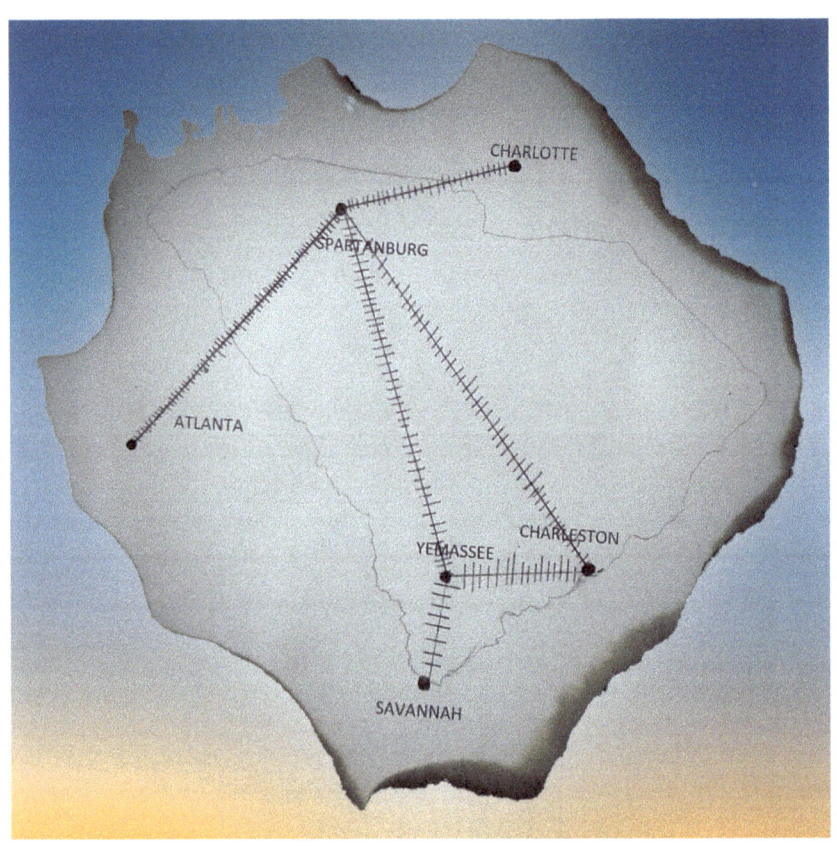

South Carolina Rail System at the turn of the 19th Century

South Carolina Waterways highlighting Black Mingo

ACKNOWLEDGMENTS

Nell would like to thank the many family members for their contributions to her first novel and for their love and support during the writing of *Black Mingo*.

Having started over twenty years ago, Nell first gives credit to her daughter, Anna, who drew the picture of Raimee and Jeannie dancing at the Coosawhatchie Juke Joint at the age of just six years old. And to her sons, Scott and Phillip, for their advice in the book's development and starting the publishing process of this book. Her three children (her three musketeers as often referred to) traveled along on many trips to the Low Country where Nell often vacationed.

Nell recognizes her two sisters, Ann, whom the family endearingly calls Sissy, and Julie, who uncannily can remember days of old, for their tremendous contributions with thoughts and direction, aiding in the flow of the writing and for the countless hours spent on the phone listening to and encouraging Nell to keep on going. *Black Mingo* could not have been written without their support.

Nell's brother, Lynn, who is inspiration for a few characters in *Black Mingo* and a future sequel book *Mingo Runs Red*, is the anchor in their family and is adored greatly.

To Aunt Janie, who is the family historian and knows a plethora of family history; she is owed a huge gratitude of thanks. Her endless stories have never disappointed.

To her special cousins Eugene, Janet, and Will, for helping to recall family stories and the countless car rides they endured for Nell to be inspired by the many places in their community of the Low Country of South Carolina.

To Uncle Wallace, who cited geographic areas, waterways, and locales, and carefully weighed in on the surnames used in her writing.

To her cousin Honey, who through the years, encouraged Nell with compliments about her writing and urged her to put pen to paper.

Nell's dearest friend, Wendy, more like a sister, who has always supported her wild and crazy ideas, her out-of-the-box thinking, and has been along for the ride on this wave of life for over thirty years now, a thank-you just doesn't seem sufficient.

Nell thanks her husband, Bo, for sacrificing hours of time that they could have spent together, when Nell would escape into her *lair* as Ann calls it. The *lair* has been Nell's refuge; her place to write, to daydream, and to create *Black Mingo*.

PROLOGUE

I have often heard it said that there is something mystical round the trees found growing on the banks of the Black Mingo. When I was a youngin, those trees had limbs that looked like they stretched out for what seemed miles, almost looked like arms trying to find their place in this world but only able to sway with the winds help.

Tales come out from down round those parts too. Like the time Jeanie, my mama, had just been paid one Friday afternoon, and she and her two girlfriends went down to Coosawhatchie to hunt up some young marine she had recently taken a fancy to. Some fella most countryfolk just called Raimee. Raimee was dressed in one of the fatigue-green uniforms that all the young boys that were called off to fight in *The Big One* were wearing, except his had sergeant stripes on both the shoulders. Guess he was trying to show somebody that he was a somebody 'cause he came walking into that dance hall with a cocky kind of look and with a walk that only Raimee could do. He came with Johnny, another country boy who had been drafted at the same time, but he wasn't so lucky getting stripes. All he got was a gun and a free boat ride to somewhere off in the South Pacific. Johnny was pretty much a youngin too, sent off to killing folks, not really trained properly but sent off anyway.

Jeanie, as she was known to all those folks, went inside that hot, steamy dance hall and, immediately, her eyes caught Raimee's outline. He was already staring at her. He couldn't help it. She was dressed that night in a red corduroy dress that flared out just right when he would go and give her a big twirl. That was a picture logged in his memory that he would call on for the rest of his life.

Jeanie and Raimee quickly connected. They danced a while, then made their way out the back screened door and took off down the bank to where the widest part of the Coosaw ran. Jeanie and Raimee, well, he ended up being my paw, had been dancing and falling in love all at the same time. Raimee picked Jeanie up to give her another twirl, and before either of them knew it, Jeanie's pocketbook, made of real alligator hide, of course filled with her full weeks' pay, ended up flying off her shoulder and into the dark, deep running waters of the Coosaw.

Just like that old river to swallow up somebody's means and not aiming to give it back. Raimee perched up high on the edge of the old concrete bridging and was getting ready to go in after that *alligator*, but Jeanie wouldn't let him. Too many bad tales about folks going into that river and not ever coming out again. Nope, just let it be. Just let it be.

Jeanie and Raimee ended up getting married later that year in the Graham Village Episcopal Church. And I came along years later. In fact, there were four of us—three girls and a boy—that they brought into this old world. Well, between those two, and all their kinfolk, my life as a child was filled with all sorts of tales from down around Black

Mingo. But none ever compared to the tale that my Aunt Ann de'Wees would end up telling me as an adult. And only then did she tell me because we had stumbled upon something—*the diary*—accidentally. Somehow that word *accidentally* seemed to follow folks who came in contact with Black Mingo, that Coosaw River.

Through cautious and carefully planned-out wording, Ann de'Wees Allen began telling the story she had not spoken of in many a year, a story that both intrigued and frightened us to this very day.

Drawing by Anna Caroline Boone Poole, 1998

CHAPTER 1

Beginnings

An unusually warm day in the Low Country of South Carolina it was, with a gentle breeze drifting across the land of sandy lanes and paths carved out long ago that Silas knew all too well.

Silas welcomed this warmer weather, brief as it may be, as the cold winter months had begun to take their toll on his now dry, cracked hands, chapped lips, and reddened cheekbones. It would not be long before winter took on the elements of an early spring, when the shortened daylight hours would turn into much longer sunup to sundown days; but for now, Silas would relish in the moments of this day.

Having just put away the weathered brown-leather saddle from a long ride on Boston, the day had really only just begun. Yet Silas felt as though he had already worked a day and then some.

Boston was the oldest, but still a middle-aged stallion, of Mister Sonders O'Ree's team; mostly comprised of Percheron horses; a breed of heavy-draft horses recently brought over from France. Boston was usually the one

Mister O'Ree called for when it was time for him to do anything outside. And it was always Silas whom Sonders depended on to make sure Boston was brushed, fed, saddled properly, straps tightened just so, and ready for him to mount and at any given time of the day or night.

But today was different. Today started before the sun of orange and yellow and bright rays of morning's first light came up from behind the eastern horizon. Sonders was heading into Yemassee and that meant Silas would be going too. It was today that without question, Sonders had to arrive at least forty-five minutes before the town clock bellowed out its clanging announcement that it was officially now 6:00 a.m.

Sonders and all his house slaves had been astir for hours, before Boston was finally mounted and ridden into town. They cantered through chilly spots of low-lying air that lurked between rows of pines and massive oaks, and a branch trickling the cold waters of her origin somewhere way off to the west from here could faintly be heard.

With the sliver of a half-moon still hanging low in the early morning sky, arriving by 5:15 a.m. assured Sonders of enough time to be sure he was already in town to make sure he was situated at the station and to be seen by those milling around the town square at such an hour.

Excitement brewed in Sonders' gut, giving him a slight buzz, all the while making him feel a bit queasy on the stomach, but it was all worth it. Sonders' hands quivered, along with the rest of his body while sitting atop of Boston and watching and waiting and listening for that first sound of arrival of Yemassee Engine 909.

CHAPTER 2

Caroleena

In a world of aristocracy, finery, privilege, debutante balls, wealth, the lack for nothing allowed the Lumford family to find themselves perching on top of the world, their world of being the cream of society.

Here this young twenty-five-year-old growing town of Spartanburg, South Carolina, was treasured by the Lumfords. Having such society, her fine citizenry, and the booming railroad startup simply showcased her wealth and her place to the not-so-faraway cities of Atlanta, Charlotte, and Charleston, and to the rest of the South. This was their world as they knew it; the world that made Spartanburg the Grand Lady of upstate South Carolina.

The larger plantations found their places in the Low Country, where hot-and-sticky days lent to the bigger and better crops of cotton, rice, sugarcane, hemp, and tobacco; but upstate South Carolina did not disappoint on this grand stage. One of the South's largest and biggest producers of both cotton and tobacco was Majestic Oaks Plantation; and here she commanded the stage with her reputation preceding herself in upstate South Carolina as the best.

Majestic Oaks Plantation was a sprawling twelve-thousand-acre home to its nine hundred slaves—give or take some, allowing for births and deaths—who took to their residency there. Sad to look at life this way, but the ebbs and flow and management of such a life was viewed just like that. It's a business. A livelihood. A way of life. And this wasn't going to change anytime soon.

Majestic Oaks Plantation was home to Atticus, Rosalyn, and Caroleena Lumford. Atticus, owner of and a hardworking overseer—the Planter—to Majestic Oaks Plantation, along with his beautiful wife, Rosalyn, by his side, had inherited the sprawl from his father, who had inherited the same land from his father. Rosalyn was as beautiful as any woman a man ever laid eyes on; until the day Caroleena entered their world and overnight seemed to have grown into the young mistress of Majestic Oaks Plantation.

Caroleena had been their only child, though the Lumfords had tried and prayed for years for more children. Needless to say, Caroleena was doted on, was given everything by everyone; and most of the times, for no reason at all, especially by Mannie, her wet nurse, her surrogate mother. When Mother wasn't around to play or pretend or dream, Mannie was her everything. Caroleena took to the doting, expecting it, expecting that she could have everything, could have it all. And that she did.

Personality of the devil was how most saw Caroleena. She was always talked about, at least behind her back, and never so that Mister Atticus or sweet dear Rosalyn could overhear. An imp. A mischief. A rascal. Trouble. Caroleena's true side showed up one rainy afternoon, just as crops were being planted and colder winter's days turned warmer and longer and supposedly brighter.

Mistress Rosalyn was in that way and was having a heap of trouble that afternoon. Nobody and nothing was aiding in her relief or delivery. Hours passed. Finally, the cries from not one but two babies bellowed from Mistress's chamber. Caroleena was not to be found. Caroleena had escaped into nowhere on Lucifer, her jet-black horse that rode like the wind. She resented that Mother had done this to her, to her world, to ruin everything that she had planned out. She hated Mother for this. And she hated Father. Plans began in her mind to set this straight and soon.

The tragic news only stoked and stirred Caroleena's brooding and hot anger—the news that Mother had passed; she had not survived her childbearing this late in life. Caroleena would be forced into a place of unrealistic expectations to help care for these two strangers now living in her house, at her Majestic Oaks Plantation.

Father had promised her great responsibility with the reward of Majestic Oaks Plantation, all of it. None of it to be shared with two sniveling brats, not on her watch nor under her care. She would see to it. Somehow. Someway. These little monsters would not have anything of hers!

Time floated quickly into years. Twins Genevieve and Priscilla grew under the care of Mannie, Caroleena's biggest loss and disappointment of all. And with Mother gone, Caroleena had been helping manage Majestic Oaks Plantation as Father turned to what he thought best: the bottle. Father's drinking consumed his morning hours, the afternoons' time, and the evenings' shadows.

Caroleena resented and hated everything and everyone. Plotting now was her only clear choice. As she had no other choice but to fulfil her devious plans.

Seventeen years of living had pushed Caroleena to leave, to escape, to say goodbye to all the things and places and people who had brought her so much pain, at least by the way she saw it through blurred, skewed eyes. Caroleena left upstate South Carolina and Majestic Oaks Plantation and Father and Genevieve and Priscilla and her Mannie and any good memory that she could have had and boarded the train for Philadelphia.

Entering the Young Ladies' Academy of Philadelphia in 1794, the first chartered institution for the higher education of young women in the United States, and perhaps the world at that time, Caroleena walked into halls of new hopes and possibilities so different to her imagination than dreaming could have ever made possible. Adjusting to a new home, temporary as it would be, having to be cordial to the other girls, and putting on the façade of being "one of them" was a challenge, but one Caroleena was up to the task to make happen. Daily classes and periodic exams were the expected. The idiocy and silliness of girls was the entertainment but was also the education Caroleena appreciated the most; she would not become one of "those" refined ladies; she would use select behaviors to build the woman she wanted to be, that she needed to be. Her dreams and goals depended on it.

An unexpected turn of events was meeting him—Desmond Osgood. A banker. A politician in the making. Wealth of Philadelphia society. Purebred aristocrat. A handsome man in all ways. Someone whom Caroleena could see making a life with as short as that may be. Schemes and goals always supersede anything that might get in her way.

Desmond was quickly taken with Caroleena. Her looks, her wit, her ambitions, all aligning with his own life's plans. Caroleena consumed every breath he took, every thought he had. Desmond was bewitched by Caroleena Lumford. And because he needed her more than he wanted her, and he needed her desperately, Desmond would take Caroleena for his wife. And, as soon as possible, make him a father to carry on his legacy.

Two train tickets to Spartanburg with gold bands on fingers signified a change in the tides. Fanfare and parties, and looks and leers, and drunkenness and jealousy greeted the newly wedded couple, just as Caroleena had envisioned, had hoped for. Not much change. Not much at all. Twin dolls bigger but lacking in any real sustenance. Mannie, now in a grave, but who cared? Not Caroleena. Majestic Oaks Plantation was not as bright and shiny as it once was but understandably as to how she got here through circumstances and time.

Father was an older and weaker man and certainly affected more by the alcohol than by elapsed time itself; neither a friend to him. Caroleena introduced Desmond to everyone who came and went, with no particular desire for Father to approve. It didn't matter. Plans would be carried out.

A matter of days into their new start of life, Father and Desmond took to the upstairs parlor, arguing, presumably about Caroleena. With glass-shattering sounds and loud voices filling the halls, Caroleena's plan had commenced. Father and Desmond pushed and shoved and power-fought over her. With the opportunity presenting, the handrail of the spiral staircase, now just fingertips' reach away, was all she needed. Pretense to caring, Caroleena edged closer, just in time to trip Father as he was near the top oak step and as his drunken body, in a slow-motion fall, proceeded to tumble. Desmond frantically reached for him, latching on, just in time for Caroleena to end Desmond as well. She did not want to succumb to Desmond's nightly advances of wanting to start a family. She was her own self. Not a mother. Not a body to carry another human, to take away her thunder, her plan. Desmond had to go too. Rolling and tumbling and screaming down each step, the two men fell to their deaths.

Nothing else to keep her here, tied to this lifeless place at Majestic Oaks Plantation, selling it all was the next designing step to Caroleena's own advancement. Taking all proceeds, she left Geneviève and Priscilla (twin brats as she now saw them) destitute and in poverty for the rest of their lives. Caroleena didn't love, didn't care, had no conscience, never thought again about what would become of the twin brats or this place.

The only road to her next chapter was Charleston. And here Caroleena's plan worked as perfectly as if she had written it for a play and actors were performing—line by line—exactly as she had written it in her imaginings.

And at the turn of the century, turn of a new year, Caroleena Lumford Osgood dreamed—no, rather burned—for the hopes of what changes in time would lend her. Walking along the market square street, close to the midnight hour of December 31, 1799, refreshed, revived, and ready for a new dawn, Caroleena would enjoy the fireworks this night as much as she had when first seeing them in Philadelphia. But tonight was different. It felt strangely odd to be here but oh so right. With thundering ruptures and vibrant colors of lights from the fireworks, Caroleena turned around to glance, to see this display of commemoration of a new year, a new century, the turn of a new page, and her eyes locked on him.

CHAPTER 3

Preacher Man

In screams of suffering and deep pants of pain, and in life's final breath, Estella O'Ree gave birth to a rather large but healthy baby boy. His first cries overshadowed the waning of sound from his momma as one life was taken for another life to live.

Mordecai and Estella O'Ree had agreed before the Lord to give their baby the surname of her father and the middle name of his father. So as Mordecai took up his newborn son into his arms and raised him up to heaven, ensuring that those around his now-deceased wife's body could see, he proclaimed the baby's name to be Sonders Josiah O'Ree.

Tears and torment began that day and would continue for the duration of Mordecai's life. Losing his wife, Estella, and now left to raise a newborn baby without a mother, all the while knowing his responsibility as the communal preacher, Mordecai felt truly alone and desperate and scared. His claim of faith in the Lord was completely different on his inside than what others who had heard Mordecai preach knew him to be on the outside. You see, Mordecai preached a good talk, but in the deepest of truth and acknowledgment to himself, he knew he did not walk that talk.

Mordecai had been lonely for months now since Estella had been in the motherly way and could not meet his physical needs. His insides ached, and he yearned deeply for a woman's touch, a returned spark of desire to fill that deepest part of one's insides; where the union of a man to a woman was the only answer to his deep, scorching need.

With no other place to turn, and within hours of Estella's death, Mordechai was at the door of his only brother, Barnabas O'Ree, begging and pleading with him to sell him one of his dispensable slave girls; one who could meet the needs of his newborn son and, without saying it aloud, Mordecai knew he would use this creature to relieve himself of his sexual desires, now long in arrears.

Barnabas O'Ree knew he had no choice but to sell property to his brother; the child's life depended on it. And so deciding, Barnabas merchandised Mordecai a female slave that needed new hope and a fresh start. The sale was Hattie. She would serve this purpose well.

Hattie was beautiful and young enough and a nurturing slave girl who just had miscarried; probably because of the physical assault she had suffered at the hands of Mr. Frederick Barber, the head slave captain at Oak Ridge Plantation. Given a little more reign from Barnabas than he should have taken, Barber was a mean, hot-tempered captain who took his rage out on a few choice slaves at Oak Ridge Plantation, and on one particular slave girl—Hattie. The beatings were hard enough to endure; but the added sexual pleasure that Barber seemed to enjoy, well, that was beyond what Barnabas would tolerate. No more!

Not knowing the deviant side of his brother, Barnabas took what he thought, the opportunity to give Hattie a new start, a different chance in this life as human property simply being owned by someone else that was free—Mordecai. Hattie would live with Mordecai and Sonders at the Graham Village Episcopal Church parsonage. Little did Hattie know, she was trading one life of misery and captivity for a new life of wretchedness and pain.

Hattie settled in quickly to her role as wet nurse to Sonders. It helped take her mind off the torture she had unfortunately grown to know all too well and all too frequently, and the silent pain deep in her soul for the child she had just recently lost was just a bit camouflaged when she held this tiny but big bundle of little baby boy close to her breast, Sonders.

On the outside, it all looked well. Someone was there now to mother Sonders. Someone there to cook, to tend to the parsonage while Mordecai was out preaching the Word of God. But inside those walls was brewing a rupture of monthslong burn for release, for a moment's assuage to his tormenting soul. His flesh burning red hot. Feelings soaring out of control. All reason and right thinking was put inside the top drawer of Mortdecai's conscience and into this emotional dresser. Do as I say! Not as I do! He knew he was a hypocrite. His actions were now in direct opposition to his *Pharisee-Sadducee* words on any given Sunday morning. But Mortdecai had fought these feelings for weeks now; he had to at least let her settle in a bit was his thinking, get used to the way things were now, and soon would be for a long, long time.

That night, in the quiet and stillness of the parsonage, just after dusk, the evening meal replete, Sonders quieted for the moment, Mordecai pounced. Taking her was easy; she was small and didn't put up a fight, and in a blurred few minutes of sick, sinful, distorted passion, Mordecai committed an act that he knew God would detest. And he would detest himself even more, for he would never forgive himself for this. But that wouldn't stop him from the repeated times of taking Hattie, night after night, bathing her body in his sweat and his seed, and to his growing disgust of himself and for her. The tainted soul of Preacher Man could not halt him from going back time and time again to his Hattie. Mordecai's appetite was insatiable. When it came to his thirst for her, his disgusting, unquenchable desires overpowered any good he could ever be now or could ever know. Preacher Man's words indicted his own morality; Mordecai's actions stole the very life, Hattie's life. God have pity on his soul.

Mordecai grew cold, distant, and more abusive, and as unloving a father as any man was ever known to be. It all stopped the day Hattie turned up with child; her baby fathered by a White man; not just any White man but the Preacher Man. The shame, the looks, the guilt would all be too much for Mordecai to mentally handle, much less if this all came to light. With no other way out of this trap, one that he laid for himself, he begged his brother, Barnabas, and his wife, Emma, to take Hattie back, along with her unborn child, and to adopt Sonders as well.

It didn't take a lot of convincing as Barnabas and Emma were still grieving the loss of their little boy, Jenkins, only eighteen months old at the time, who succumbed to a horrible sickness of high fever and shaking chills, heart arrhythmia, sore throat, and rash, eventually closing off his ability to breathe at all. Gasping for each breath, holding Jenkins in their arms, forever holding a piece of their heart, his little lifeless body took over the existence of their happy, bouncing, little boy. A century later, this sickness would be diagnosed as *diphtheria*, taking thousands of lives, particularly children. Never having any other children, Barnabas and Emma eagerly welcomed adopting Sonders from Mordecai.

What sort of father could Mordecai ever be? The little bit of decency left in Mordecai gave him the courage to do what was best, to put an end to this sick, depraved way of living. Get rid of it all, once and for all.

CHAPTER 4

Brothers

This was the easy part. Growing up beside his brother. Or as some said half-brother, but it didn't make any never mind who said it or what was said. Skin color was just that—skin deep. He was his blood brother. They were the best of friends. Nothing would ever stand between these two. Absolutely nothing.

Sonders was just eleven months and two weeks old when little bit Silas came into his world. They were like twins, acted like it, joined at the hip, some would say, with their every move and care in the world. They were entwined. Barnabas and Emma O'Ree didn't seem to mind so much; Sonders was well taken care of by their Hattie, now come home and without the fear of Barber around anymore. He was long gone. Barnabas had seen to that. So the O'Ree's simply let Hattie raise *her boys* however time would take them or however events would mold them.

Sonders was smart and kind, gentle and thoughtful, strong and rather handsome; he was the young master of Oak Ridge Plantation in the making, but none of that compared to the bigness of his heart. The growing-up child cared for every living creature—young or old, small or large. He loved them all. He loved life, and this showed in everything he did and said. Sonders epitomized the scripture that *be not deceived; God is not mocked: for whatsoever a man soweth, that shall he also reap*—Galatians 6:7 KJV—he loved the Word of God, not because of the tainted relationship he experienced with Mordecai, now just an estranged man whom he knew was his birth father, but because Scripture was real and alive, and it moved Sonders inside and in ways that drove him daily in all that he did.

Youthful, carefree days transformed instantly for not just Sonders but for all souls living on Oak Ridge Plantation that rainy, stormy night. A brilliant sunny day and starlit dusky sky had given way the night before to a spate of gruesome displays by Mother Nature as she rained down her fury and angst on the Low Country. A half a century later, this kind of storm would be what the Low Country would know and recognize and frequently encounter all too well—a *hurricane*; for now, Sonders and Silas simply saw it as *Armageddon*.

A spate of flooding waters pushed Black Mingo to her brinks and beyond. It was the storm of all storms liken unto none the Low Country had ever experienced.

As easily and as unnoticed as a caterpillar turns into a beautiful butterfly, Sonders life transformed, like pages in a book turning over into a whole new chapter. Better yet, an entire new book of life that night. Some say it was the river; some say it was the wind of God's breath breathing down in anger; whatever happened, however it happened, whatever it was, life had ended for some, and a new life began for others.

Sometimes, only the good Lord knows why, and this was one of those times. Mister and Mistress O'Ree were out in that squall, going somewhere or coming back from something; nobody would ever know their reason. Barnabas and Emma were taken away, ripped straight out of their buggy, and into the dark, churning waters of Black Mingo.

It was the next day when the buggy was found at the crossing of what was usually the shallow edge of Black Mingo; waters still breeching her banks, running higher than the oceans' waves that Sonders had seen more than once at high tide. Their mules, Hickory and Royal, were found with broken, contorted legs and harnesses wrapped all around, twisted and knotted; everything all wrapped around the base of Uncle Henry; the biggest and oldest live oak tree found living on Oak Ridge Plantation. And it was there, along his long, unfolded limbs stretching out on top of the ground, Spanish moss dangling, dripping wet droplets from the storm now passed that they found Barnabas and Emma's lifeless bodies shrouded by Uncle Henry's arms; almost like he was trying his best to protect them, to hold them close, but unable to against the storm. What a sight it all was. In the storm of all storms, why did they have to die?

Sonders naturally took over Oak Ridge Plantation that day from Uncle Barnabas and Aunt Emma O'Ree, the plantation, a homeplace to more than 221 slaves. With crops of tobacco and mostly cotton, they hoped that the cotton still in the field had at least survived. Sonders cherished how his adoptive parents had cared for all that God had entrusted them with, and he would do the same. He would pay them back for all of their goodness and kindness and be an even better Planter to Oak Ridge Plantation, a better master to his slaves.

Sonders Josiah O'Ree. Who would have thought? Guess he knew this would happen one day but not now, not while he wasn't even a quarter of a century old yet; now Sonders found himself the sole owner, master of Oak Ridge Plantation. He had it all, except for someone to share it with, a wife by his side.

Sonders loved that Silas had not just married another slave to create more of the same at Oak Ridge Plantation; Silas had married the love of his soul, Lucy. And together they oversaw the Big House. Hattie had made sure of her conditions with Barnabas and Emma when she returned pregnant and with Sonders in tow back to Oak Ridge Plantation. Nope. Sonders wasn't jealous of Silas because he had found love, never once thought about it that way. He just simply longed for a partner of his own; a special lady, a lover, someone to be a mama to his own children and to grow old with him while making great memories and to bring real change to Oak Ridge Plantation.

Sonders hoped he could somehow be an influencer to his neighboring planters; it had to start somewhere, with someone. Sonders was going to bring change to this place, give his slaves a contract to indenture them. It may take him years and years, but it had to change. No longer did he want to possess another person. He didn't want to own people. Sonders wanted to give them a chance to make their own way in life. He knew this would not sit well with anybody he knew; but Sonders knew that Silas deserved this, a chance, and if Silas deserved it, well, then, so did they all.

Oak Ridge Plantation slaves knew Sonders. Many of them had grown up right beside of him and Silas. Sonders wasn't afraid to work right alongside them, out in the fields, from sunup to sundown. He had earned their respect out of care and love, not out of beatings and fear. Sonders had earned their love and faithfulness too.

Early winter of 1799 was turning out to be a good end to a bumpy fall, when that horrible storm wreaked its havoc on every plantation for miles and miles around, not sparing Oak Ridge Plantation or any other place that Sonders knew of. Good seed and loyal, devoted, and hard workers culminated in yielding a windfall crop of cotton. All souls at Oak Ridge Plantation were more than pleased. The cotton was ginned early, earlier than usual; it would be ready to take to market, just after Christmas this year, wouldn't have to wait till after the New Year like usual. *Armageddon* somehow didn't affect the cotton crop but seemed to have made everything somehow better.

Just to make this particular trip was always exciting, and Sonders always looked forward to the sights along this certain route. However, something stirred inside him today, something he couldn't quite understand; but God with him, he was ready for whatever would happen. Sonders and Silas and their loaded wagons took out for their journey north. With Boston hitched at the back of the wagons, he had an adventure of his own to take with Sonders once there. The Percherons, Jericho and Wilbur and Dodge and Whiskey, were ready to go, eager to pull, more than able to pull this load, acting as though they, too, knew this was going to be a fruitful trip for Oak Ridge Plantation. Snorting and pulling, their nostrils flaring with each breath, the frigid air illuminated their misty clouds of exhaled air, and so this adventure began.

With Christmas now past and loaded down wagons, Sonders and Silas knew the sixty-mile journey would cost them three days of driving the team at full maximum of their capability; had to be done; this precious load depended on beating any and all competition to the scales in Charleston, and most assuredly to be there before the first of the New Year.

The conclusion of the eighteenth century was approaching quickly. Charleston found herself as the largest port city south of Philadelphia, and a bustling trade center she was, growing faster than a tick on the back of a furry dog. The Oak Ridge Plantation team finally arrived into the busy city as did many other wealthy colonists escaping their harsh northern winters. Most of the boarding houses were filled to capacity and would certainly be stretched by their occupancy during the holiday season. Sonders fortunately found vacancy at Miriam's, a boarding house not so far from the Picker House, for the weary sojourner that colder than usual December night.

Morning's first light took both Sonders and Silas to the Picker House, not too far from the waterfront where slave trade was carried out daily. That's not what Oak Ridge Plantation had come for today; nope, cotton was the agenda for this Charlestonian trip. The two teams pulled their hefty loads up and onto the delivery ramp of the Picker House to offload their prized crop. With anticipation and excitement running through their veins, the *brothers* anxiously waited for the workhands to unpack the cotton from the bales, removing any debris from the field that Sonders' slaves had missed. Oak Ridge Plantation walked away that morning, yielding twenty cents a pound! Top dollar for the cotton market this early in the season and awarded only to the best and finest. Sonders had played this out well, was beyond pleased and proud knowing that his crop would be exported from this Charleston port and make its way up into New England and even across the oceans' waters to England. Yes, it had been a very good day.

Silas would have loved no more than to be with Sonders in this big, exciting place, tonight, of all nights, celebrating the New Year. He knew it was best for him to settle in at Miriam's, didn't want to cause any trouble for his master, his beloved brother, just because of his *difference.*

Just after the evening's meal, Sonders hesitantly left Silas and ventured out into the streets of Charleston, and into the mystery of the night's air. He didn't realize it then, but his life would be soon changed forever.

Thunderous sounds booming along the cobblestoned streets and up in the starry evening sky took Sonders farther away into the night, stumbling once on an uneven stone, then regaining his balance. Standing now sure-footedly upon the cobblestones, Sonders eyes were met with those of the most exquisite beauty he had ever seen; his heart stirred, raced; he was immediately attracted to this beautiful, dewy complexioned woman. He had to meet her. All too soon, the sky-gazing crowds caused them to lose sight of each other, much to Sonders' dismay. Had she been an apparition, a ghost? Was Sonders dreaming? He could only hope and pray that this dove was real. With all of his being, Sonders knew that his destiny would be to find her again and, soon, very soon.

CHAPTER 5

Soiree Time

Before heading back to Graham Village that next day, there was much still to do—a visit to the mercantile to purchase specific supplies that Sonders could only buy in the city, the soiree at Rutledge Plantation later that night, and his search for *her*.

Pockets full of profit, Sonders and Silas filled both wagons with field goods, like barley, feed grain, seed for planting, and some iron tools to replace a few broken ones now finding their refuge on the floor of the Woodshed, large sacks of sugar, rice, and various spices to replenish the kitchen's stockroom at the Big House, and enough cloth and threads for Lucy and her girls to sew the new, necessary clothes for Oak Ridge Plantation slaves to wear come spring. Loaded up and battened down with large leather tarps, the wagons would be safe until morning, when the teams would turn and head south for home. However, for now, Sonders had one thing on his mind, in his heart, and one thing only; that lovely creature had cast an enchanting spell on him. He had to find her, had to see her, even if it might be for the last time.

Sonders found himself wandering along the same street where he had seen her that night. The turn of the century filled now with new hope, new possibilities, new anticipations for what might be. Could he find her? Would he see her again? Sonders had confided in Silas about his special encounter, and he was as excited for his brother as he recalled discovering that his heart was meant for Lucy. Sonders searched, waited, nothing, the afternoon soon began to take on the sky tones that daylight was quickly retreating. Time had run out. Oh, he had given it his best try to find her, to see her one more time. Now all Sonders could do was return to Miriam's and ready himself for the evening's event.

The Rutledge Plantation "Ringing in the New Year" soiree was how the special-delivered, handwritten invitation had read. Sonders had known the Rutledges most of his life—good folks, probably Barnabas and Emma's closest friends. Distance is the only thing that separated them in their close friendship. It would be good to see Walter and Callie Rutledge again, under different circumstances. The last time was at Barnabas and Emma's funeral at Graham Village Episcopal Church with only a few minutes' visit out at the graveyard, laying their bodies to rest in the Lord.

Cleaning up and dressing for the soiree kept Sonders busy enough for the next little bit, but his mind was that of a different beast now, could not get her face out of his mind, could not control the racing of his heart, his breaths, even a little more heavy yet shallow. Even with the shadows of that night clouding much of his memory, and the crowded streets making it difficult to get a complete look at her, Sonders had seen enough of her and that unique beauty to be etched into his memory forever, and he would try to make her his own. However, a bit of sadness filled him with a dismay that maybe it was just a dream.

*****

She had been staying with the Rutledges since before Christmas and would be there well past the New Year celebration. Delia would see to that. Caroleena had met Walter and Callie Rutledge's oldest daughter, Delia, when they both had attended the Young Ladies' Academy of Philadelphia in 1794. Best of friends—at least Delia thought them to be. She thought better than that. They were not best friends. They were not even friends. How could someone like her have a friend? That would only circumvent her plans for everything she held high in her standards: her goals, her must-haves in life.

But turning down an invitation to stay at one of the wealthiest plantations and with one of the highest of society families in Charleston would be a big mistake. Why, it might even be her next stepping stone for advancement of her plans. Time would soon tell for sure. For now, she would go along with the masquerade of being Delia's friend, showing all the politeness, the smiles at just the right moments, the "oh my goodness" looks when need be, and would even cry on Delia's shoulder, just as a *best friend* would do. She could sob through the stories of how she had lost her mother as a young girl and the horrible accident that her father and newly wedded husband had succumbed to, that horrible accident that she knew how to tell with all the right pauses and with tears to follow, and that she had lost her twin sisters in that awful tragedy at Majestic Oaks Plantation, all gone now to the hands of fiery flames that consumed her plantation. Spartanburg had lost so much. She had lost even more. She was destitute; at least that was the lie she told the Rutledges, hoping to garner their sympathies and some compassion. All she could hope for and more was what she ended up with—a bidding to come stay with the Rutledges for as long as she would need, to come to Charleston, and that she did. And another connection to wealth and power would be at her disposal.

Staying only long enough with Delia to get settled would have to work; she could not stomach the thought of having to pretend to be her *friend* any longer than she had to, and lying wasn't hard to do at all. It was a part of who she was to get what she wanted. Charleston, the Rutledge Planation, and their way of life was the next door to make the right acquaintances and, hopefully soon, to find her next target.

Delia recognized that Caroleena had lost much over the last year—her father, her husband, her two sisters, and her home. What a horrible thing to have happened. It was Delia who suggested to Mommy and Dadda that throwing a big banquet or party was in order to introduce her to the cream of Charlestonian society and wealth, both male and female. She needed to make new friends and find a new suitor and make a new home. This would be the first soiree of the new year, of the new century!

Caroleena had spent the afternoon strolling along the same cobblestone street, where all the festivities had been, just hours before, just before midnight. Thoughts of him cycled through her mind, like a reel of film would show centuries later. He looked perfect, looked like high society, had that air about him; the look in his eye that was returned to her ogling him was a sign that he was worth her pursuit, but she needed to find him, and she needed him in her life now.

Returning to Rutledge Plantation, Caroleena was feeling a tad defeated not having completed her mission of finding him. Her spirits lit up with the delivery neatly and nicely boxed with a satin tie to keep it closed for shipping. The box was left lying on her bed in the suite set up for special guests. Opening the box and holding the beautiful frock up to her body, Caroleena envisioned that a very special night must lie ahead.

Preparing for the soiree, she leisurely bathed, and stepped into a beautifully designed frock. It was a rushed order from Lady Louise-Marie, a seamstress newly arrived from Paris who was getting her start in the bustling settlement of New York City and trying to make her way in this new world. So she gave Louise-Marie a chance, ordered a gown, a lilac, floral silk with a tightly laced corset over a chemisette—a camisole—a bodice that fit her stunning figure, revealing just enough of her upper body, both voluptuous bosom and sensuous back, plenty of crinoline petticoats under the layers of skirting adorned with elaborate embroideries and lacy trims, all united to flare the skirt wide and flattering. It was flawless. Caroleena went into her locked trunk to select just the right piece of jewelry to accessorize.

Stepping into the gown, Caroleena ensured that she had tucked the trunk key away into privacy. Unhurried to dress, she admired herself along the journey and was rather quite pleased. Adjusting her long sunny blond locks, placing strands in just the right places to highlight her face, all held up and in place with a beautiful metal wrought haircomb with an etched creamy white magnolia blossom, accentuated her image perfectly. Taking a final glance at herself in the antique freestanding cheval mirror that stood at the door for one's last glance, it was perfect. She was perfect.

Making her way down the long hallway and to the top of the grand staircase, she sauntered. The sounds of this place alive made her insides tingle with excitement. Making one last adjustment to the skirts of her gown, Caroleena started down the staircase, stopping on the last step, eyes gazing straight ahead. How dashing, this well-dressed handsome man that she feverishly had longed to meet; it was *him*.

*****

Boston's special reason for this journey had arrived. Sonders rode Boston, his beautiful, black stallion, out to the Rutledge Plantation. Boston had made this trip before. He knew the way. Sonders settled Boston in at the stables before heading up to the Main House. With invitation in hand, Sonders was as strikingly handsome as any man here, dressed appropriately for the occasion in waistcoat and matching breeches, the lace jabot falling just below the neck, linen shirt with decorative cuffs, and, of course, a pair of silk stockings snuggled against his legs, inside neatly polished boots.

He walked up and into the Rutledge Plantation's large open oak front doors and joined in the receiving line, patiently waiting his turn. A handshake was offered to Walter first, giving Callie a gentleman's hug, and lingering a bit longer than others may have understood. Sonders pulled away and, looking up, there *she* was, standing on the lower step of the grand staircase, staring at him. Fortune or fate had entered both of their lives instantaneously and at this very moment in time.

*****

Delia reminded Mommy and Dadda what this evening meant to all of them but, most importantly, to her friend. Walter introduced the world to her that night, and Charlestonian society was laid at her fingertips. "Ladies and gentlemen, I am pleased to introduce to you, to our Charleston society, *Caroleena Lumford Osgood.*"

*****

It was then he heard her name for the very first time as Walter introduced this beauty, Caroleena Lumford Osgood. What a lovely name for such a beautiful woman.

Sonders urged Walter to introduce him, this woman whose image had captured every fiber of his being. Now getting ready to officially meet her, walking nearer to her; every step brought him closer to the woman who would change Sonders' life, his world.

Immediate attraction and fiery passion at first touch, hands clasped in greeting, instantly brought these two together, both needing the other, just in completely different ways, with different needs. The chamber music playing from the small ensemble hired for such an evening as this, was prominently placed and in eye's view, but not to be a distraction from the evening's purpose or to interfere with the soiree. The air's melody intertwined their souls. Caroleena and Sonders danced the night away, not stopping but only to wait for the next waltz to begin, their bodies so close, their minds locked on one another, cementing emotions and needs that very night. They both knew it. They both needed this. A happy new year to all and a new grand century ahead for sure.

Gazing into each other's eyes, they forgot about all the other guests dancing around them. The two characters were obviously smitten with one other; she for Sonders' wealth that he exuded, and he for Caroleena's beauty of her demure composure. The night was filled with magic for them both. Dancing and swaying to the music, the night passed by all too quickly. By the end of the evening, they both knew this would only be the beginning of their delirious love affair. Their evening was sealed with their first passionate kiss, a rupture of delight and visions of fireworks that had first brought their wandering paths along cobblestone streets into a parallel line with one another.

Sonders remained in Charleston, sending Silas back with the wagons. Caroleena would say goodbye forever to the Rutledge Plantation, to Delia, and to that sort of life as she had found her next project. Sonders and Caroleena's union was but a mere one month later. He would give her his world, and she greedily would take it.

CHAPTER 6

Oak Ridge Plantation
The Big House

Sonders had heard so many stories growing up from Barnabas and Emma, and even Hattie, as to how Oak Ridge Plantation came to be; and that there was no other estate around to be compared or any grander a place that anyone had ever seen.

Sonders had just recently inherited the plantation after the tragic accident of Uncle Barnabas and Aunt Emma O'Ree, and he was glad he knew its history well. This sprawling parcel came down to Barnabas from his father, Haymoth O'Ree; and it was Haymoth's father, Allister O'Ree, who began construction on the Big House in the year of our Lord 1691.

His great-grandfather Allister had procured his first group of this kind of property with sixty-eight chattel slaves, human beings equated with livestock, possessions, owned souls. It was then he knew that his dream could then become a reality. Slave trade was an already thriving business in the new world with over forty percent of all enslaved Africans coming to North America entering through Charlestonian waters and her port. Allister's first order of business was to build his dream, an opulent and as lavish a house as anyone had ever seen; one that would, without a question, be the grandest of all homes in the New World, America.

Oak Ridge Plantation required a dominant, established residence for the Planter, Allister, and his wife, Cora, and their family to live in once built. Allister called it the Big House. It would be his home, the center of his sprawling estate, an architectural wonder of its day, a showpiece to anybody and everybody who might travel those parts of the new world to see, to take in the sights of a working, successful, and productive plantation, its crops, the newness of the business of slavery, and his wealth and power that he saw himself attaining, and that he did.

Allister did not need envy or any jealousy from anyone. He received all accolades for his longings; he wanted to be a leader, a spokesman for such a life, wanted to see growth and development and prosperity in that land, in the new province of Carolina. This region would officially become South Carolina, the eight state of the Union in 1788. Oak Ridge Plantation was to be a demonstration of a functioning estate; not just a home but a business, a new way of life to all who lived nearby and afar, and it succeeded that goal by more than could be imagined.

Allister O'Ree's slaves spent their first year and a half scavenging for oysters from the marshy banks and river bottoms of the Broad River at low tide near Port Royal Sound. Oysters thrived in salty or brackish coastal waters and that made for the ideal environment for them, and that was the perfect place, the coastal waters found only miles away from Oak Ridge Plantation. Allister's vision was made possible. He had real hope.

With teams of oxen and large-spoke wheeled, flat-bedded wagons, day after day, week after week, Allister's slaves hauled literally hundreds upon thousands of oysters up to Oak Ridge Plantation. Thank the Lord for Black Mingo, the river that ran alongside Oak Ridge Plantation; it made dragging and hauling the shell loads a wee bit easier for those working tirelessly, a task not easily taken but done anyway. Slave women and young children spent their days shucking the oyster from each shell, tender hands bled and knuckles made raw, providing enough food during those long months to feed the whole lot of folks living on Oak Ridge Plantation.

Nobody went hungry around there, except maybe for a time or two and only every so often, when somebody simply just got tired of eating oysters stewed, fried, steamed, baked, or raw; the meat had filled many a belly. Shell heaps piled up everywhere but were always placed strategically around each pier footing of the Big House. It came to life right before all eyes of everyone connected to Oak Ridge Plantation; at three stories high, it would be looked upon as the most palatial and beautiful home anywhere around, then and now and for a long time to come.

All those oyster shells had a specific part to play, their part in the building of the Big House. Once floor joists and exterior walls had been established upon the piers, each oyster shell nestled neatly and into their place and became the veneer of the Big House, gracing this place with its one-of-a-kind look. Nowhere else on God's green earth was there such a beauty. Allister had his vision, his plan, and his process all laid out in his mind, while slaves had given that vision life, but with their blood, their sweat and, for a few, their lives.

When completed, the Big House seemed as though it had a face-like resemblance; it looked like it had eyes staring back at you with a nose and a mouth and maybe even a beard. The oyster shells, with their rough texture and irregular shape, gave the veneer its creamy, whitish-gray coloring; the long, glass-paned windows and huge oak door, all still right there, was the Big House's eyes and nose; and for a mouth and beard, the giant front porch wrapped clear around its face, going out of eyesight on both sides, grinning-like, stopping where stone steps reached the entrance to the backdoor of the detached kitchen and mammoth-sized, rock-faced fireplace. It was a beauty. No one would or could ever disagree about that.

Two story flanker buildings were erected, one to the left and one to the right of the magnificent home with curving, cloistered, tabby walls connecting themselves to the Big House. Tabby was made up special like from lime collected from burned oyster shells and mixed in with sand, water, ash, and other shells. The two smaller homes served the estate as additional sleep lodges, still do—one for very special guests, the other for house slaves responsible for early rise and late night work inside the Big House, serving the Planter and his family's needs, even to this day.

Rumors are always embellished, and almost a hundred years later, purportedly, a president of the United States had been traveling through the area, heading toward Savannah, and that he would stay at this grand beauty, probably because there were no other boarding houses nearby for him to overnight. It was in 1791 that President George Washington apparently took a bed and rested his weary body from a long day's travel for the night at Oak Ridge Plantation; an honor bestowed on the sprawling estate and to the O'Rees; and for their local settlement of Graham Village, an honor that provided them notoriety and societal gains in this community, which would one day explode with reputation and prestige. Surely the O'Rees must have been the finest host and hostess to such a regal visitor.

The Big House overlooked and oversaw the entire plantation from where it had been built, and it finally started its purpose. This was good, but there were areas around the ten-thousand-acre homestead that were secret to only Oak Ridge Plantation, that weren't quite so beautiful, not so perfect, or so adored. There was a place that most dared not to go. They would go but only because they had to.

CHAPTER 7

The Woodshed

Don't know if those sounds coming out of the small, crooked, and battered wooden door were howls and cries from what must have happened behind those walls at some point or if imagination simply echoed what one might think a poor soul could possibly utter while enduring such excruciating pain. All that matters now is that sort of punishment doesn't happen around here anymore. Things were going to change.

Sonders wasn't going to let it happen on his watch. Nope. Fair treatment was what he cared about. He saw his property as part of his family, a part of his inheritance, his heritage, his legacy. Just like Silas was his brother—well, brother by the same father, just by another mother—all the brown-skinned destined folks living at Oak Ridge Plantation were his pride, his joy, and now his responsibility. And he was going to take care of them extra special-like. Slaves were the backbone to any plantation, no matter what any of his neighbors said, particularly his father, the Preacher Man, Mordecai O'Ree.

The Woodshed was now home to farming equipment waiting their turn to be used and broken furniture but still some good parts needing to be built into something else worthwhile. Crates of Uncle Barnabas O'Ree's notes from previous years' cotton sales and bills of sale for the 221 slaves that Sonders now owned, all stacked up in the corner, perfectly and pointedly out of view. That was what this place was for now, only good going forward, not for what it had been built for, the place for punishment.

Not too many moons ago, the Woodshed had been a place of fear, disgust, and terror, and was all at the hands of Mr. Frederick Barber. Barber was Barnabas's head slave captain, overseer of the slaves; though Barnabas gave Barber some leniency, he was clueless as to the destructive nature and evil cruelty that Barber held inside his soul. The occasional tying a rebellious, not-working-hard-enough slave to the whipping tree out in the work yard so that all slaves could witness a potential judgment was just that—occasional; and Barnabas was okay with what needed to be done in order to maintain rule and order with his property. A whipping was just a common way to punish, to discipline, always with clothing removed, except for the female slave only had to disrobe down to the waist but, nonetheless, exposing her naked breasts for all eyes to see.

But what Barnabas did not know was that there were several slaves Barber had contempt for, for some reason or another, unleashing cruel and unusual and unrealistic wrath upon, not just punishment, and that was conducted inside the Woodshed. It was there where Barber would whip and nearly mutilate the backs of some of the more robust, stronger male slaves to the point of them looking like limp, splintered pulpwood, useless for days and on into weeks ahead, sometimes until their backs would heal up, only to be submitted once again to the torture Barber knew all too well how to unleash. Great pleasure was wrought by reopening wounds, scars and scabs, bleeding and oozing and deepening the scarring with Barber's lost compass of morality and with each blow he could strike with his whip.

But it was in the Woodshed that Barber would privately and secretively take young Hattie, binding her hands with the rusty, iron shackles teethed tightly into the cracked and splintered wooden board fastened securely into the wall of the Woodshed. It was in that corner, dark and musty and shadowed, that hidden place where no one would know and no one would dare go.

Hattie's back would be pressed into the wood, splintering pieces of wall, metal digging into her wrists as Barber would take her over and over again, using her body for the pleasures that he took at her expense. Thrusting and pushing and forcing his body into her, Barber brutally tortured this young slave girl, and for no real reason. Daring her to scream or to make a sound only added to his deviant hunger. Hattie knew all too well than to scream. She had suffered Barber's more brutal attack when she shrieked that first time. With fists and booted feet kicking, Barber raged until Hattie passed out, hanging by her wrists for however long, escaping the pain, fleeing the fear, dodging reality if only for a moment. Hattie had found another place in her subconscious mind—a safe place to run to. This was the reality Hattie would get to know and, all too soon. It was her fate for now, at the hands of Mr. Frederick Barber.

With force and rapidity building in each thrust, Barber would cover Hattie; his climax finishing with a final and sickening groan. It was then that Barnabas walked in and found this scene playing out before him. Rushing to release this poor child from the grips of fear and pain and abuse, Barnabas' face of shock and disgust told Barber that this would be the last time.

Her body covered in his discharge, her full nakedness, tears streaming down her shattered face, Barnabas held the girl in his arms. It was obvious that she had been with child, and that cycle was now over, ended. The lifeless stillbirth of a forming baby lay on the dirt floor of the Woodshed. Barnabas' eyes rushed back and forth from Hattie to Barber. Barnabas yelled to get out, to leave this place, and to never show his face on Oak Ridge Plantation ever again. This miscarriage of life was what had allowed Hattie to become Sonders' wet nurse, just weeks after her loss.

Seeing the Woodshed each and every day was a reminder to Sonders of his Uncle Barnabas' directives, though, how to be good and fair, all the while maintaining order, setting the example, keep control. It was an absolute necessity. That one corner of the Woodshed was not to be shunned nor to feel bad about but must be kept in full view for all who walked by it daily or through its door to see, to reflect upon, or so he said. Sonders didn't want to think about that cruelty, at least the way he saw it. Those days, that time on Oak Ridge Plantation was now in the past once and for all.

CHAPTER 8

Preparation Day

Long before the roosters made their declaration of another day at Oak Ridge Plantation, the Big House was coming to life as if all by herself, by the very breath needing to fill its lungs. Each room began to echo its own distinction, discerning one from the next by senses of sight and smells and sounds.

Earlier lit logs were already leaving their embers in the fireplaces that were found throughout the house, bringing both warmth and fragrance that is unique to them and them alone. The smell of bacon frying up, bread baking in the large open-faced fireplace, and strong brewing coffee gave the grand kitchen an aroma unique to each and every new morning.

The faint sound of clanking china dishes and bowls announced this was their special day as each piece was lifted from its nestled spot in the massive oak hutch that had stood in its same place in the grand dining room for well over a hundred years. The cushion-lined cedar box of all the many different pieces of silver tinkled as to their awakening as each piece was delicately lifted from their burrowed hole to await being shined once more, to be used once again.

This was the early morning production of the Big House slaves overseen by Silas and his wife, Lucy. Everything would be in place and on time and just perfectly so-so, for there was no room for error on this particular day at Oak Ridge Plantation.

The busyness around the house was almost dizzying, what with each room in the house abuzz with activity. Lucy moved quickly from the dining room to the kitchen to the master bedroom to the foyer, only to do it all over and over again. Lucy was watching every small detail come to life, just as she and Mister O'Ree had talked it over time after time after time. And now she could see their plans coming to life right before her eyes.

The large pottery crock bowls were standing ready nearby the hot wood stove that would be filled with fluffy scrambled eggs and white milk sausage gravy, white fluffy biscuits large enough to cover the palm of any field man's hand, to platters for the bacon and sausage and urns waiting to be filled with hot coffee and pitchers for milk and freshly squeezed orange juice; a special treat this time of year; a luxury not only the slaves did not frequently see, but Oak Ridge Plantation residents only enjoyed a few times in their lifetimes.

The dining room was taking its shape with the freshly laundered white linen and laced-edge tablecloth draping over the top of the eight-foot-long, claw-footed oak table, made complete with the eight armless chairs and two captain's chairs pulled up underneath, awaiting to seat each their own guest. Hot mats and doilies and hand-crocheted placemats were all arranged to accommodate the special guests of honor once back home for their first meal of the day. The fine china plates handed down from at least three generations back were set out beside neatly arranged and polished silverware patterns, and cream-colored linen napkins trimmed with an ivy branch design interlocking so perfectly and lovely that no one should ever want to touch their lips to the fine cloth for fear of staining them to their ruin.

Floors were being swept, then again, just to make sure. The large elaborately designed woolen rugs in the foyer and hallways, in the dining room and bedrooms, had all been strung out between two trees in the sun for days at a time and beaten with flathead mallets at least more than a half dozen times, airing out the drab days of winter that had collected on them over the last many months of their lives.

Today, Lucy found herself fretting over the most important room in the Big House; Mister O'Ree's room, the master's bedroom. Mister's room was more massive than the other bedrooms, taking on a very different personality than all the other rooms at Oak Ridge Plantation. Located on the backside of the west wing of Oak Ridge Planation, Mister's room was high enough up to look out over his plantation, to the gentle easement, down to the banks of Black Mingo. The afternoon sun as it made its way across the sky to its settling place just over the western horizon, always left Mister's room plenty warm, even on the chilliest days of the year.

As Lucy entered Mister's bedroom, she stopped and recalled the days when she was little, having played in the house as her own mother who once managed the Big House was off minding all to be done in and around the place. This room had been her favorite. Back then, it had been Barnabas O'Ree's room, the prior master of Oak Ridge Plantation and Sonders' uncle. Lucy and other house slaves played and sometimes hid under the bed, falling asleep on cloudy, rainy afternoons.

On the largest wall in Mister's room stood the massive, grand fireplace that fed both his room and the adjoining en-suite boudoir that would be kept for the lady of the house; that is, once Sonders met the love of his life to bring into his home. Lucy could almost imagine the heat this fireplace could produce, and the heat from passion later tonight that would come.

CHAPTER 9

Homecoming

This time of year, when cold winter months begin taking on the element of warmer springlike days, mornings meet with a cool crisp air, and sandy, rutted lanes and paths are alit with sunny bright rays lying low to the ground, warming the Low Country down to her underbelly, low-down, deep within the layers upon layers of sandy soil, waiting for new life to awaken into all sorts of forms of life. Buds pop their heads up through the soil, and creatures of all kinds find their way toward their purpose, their calling in life. God just does it this way. The cycles in life. Something has to die so that new life can take death's place.

The Big House was bustling with activity and excitement; Lucy was anticipating the arrival of Mister and Lady, his new wife, to Oak Ridge Plantation. She had instructed the house slaves on their various duties, gathering clipped late-winter, early-spring dianthus, purplish-blue violas, varied-colored, face-like pansies, lavender Bergenia, purple foxglove, and clusters of creamy dusty miller flowers from the garden and arranged in lovely urns and crystal vases to be dispersed but placed just so, all around the many rooms of the Big House. They would serve their purpose of a heartfelt welcome this morning; and later that night, their purpose would be the special decoration to help brighten each room, once guests arrived.

Extra polish was used for the furniture to gleam bright so as one could see their reflection peering back, rugs beaten and floors swept yet once again kept everyone busy; and the delicious morning food being prepared alongside the evening's banquet meal gave the Big House a unique and inviting aroma to all who entered her doors. Not a thing would be out of place, not a detail left undone.

Stopping only to take a couple of good breaths and to preview the result of all her labors of the day, Lucy's thoughts were interrupted by old Roscoe and Jasper, childhood hunting dogs of Sonders; their barking bellowing loudly outside, louder than thunder clapping, just before a devil of a storm, announcing an arrival.

Lucy was particularly excited, not only because Mister had found his companion but also that she would be her lady's maid. Lucy hurriedly assembled the house slaves together outside the Big House, semi-circled, shoulder to shoulder, in front of the prominent, white-picketed-banister front porch, ready to meet this fair lady, Mrs. Sonders Josiah O'Ree.

A distance away, and facing the long, sandy lane approaching the Big House from the main road that lead into Graham Village, a first glimpse of a wagon was sighted, loaded with trunks and cases and escorted by two horses, Boston and Diablo, Mister's and now Lady's horses.

Lucy could hardly wait to meet the woman who Sonders had talked about endlessly this past month, of her beauty, her wit, charm, poise; her attributes were endless. She could not imagine a man more in love with a woman than Mister was, and she was so happy for him; he would be lonely no more; he had met the woman of his dreams.

*****

Silas, dutiful and loyal to his master, his friend, his brother, had stood beside Sonders and waited patiently as they met the 909; whistle blowing, steam billowing, wheels roaring and screeching to a slow stop; the engine pulled into Yemassee Station with everything Sonders now treasured. In one leap off Boston, Sonders was in no time up on the platform to greet and escort his newly wedded wife into her new life in Graham Village.

Descending steps from the wooden-planked platform, Silas watched the newlyweds, now linked arm in arm, walking quickly toward him. As if floating on a cloud, the brothers embraced heartily; Sonders smiling and motioning this beauty, this delightful creature forward, to be introduced to one another. "Silas, meet Caroleena. Caroleena, meet Silas."

In a twinkling of an eye, had Silas seen a reluctance or possibly a barely noticeable scowl on this unblemished, perfect, and lovely face as if Sonders' urging her to meet his brother was a sin, a mar, a curse? Silas quickly dismissed the notion. This day was to be perfect. There was nothing but good and fulfillment of a lifelong dream and excitement in the air. Silas busied himself with loading Lady Caroleena's trunks and cases into the wagon, while she held her parasol positioned, just so to keep the sun's rays away; but a nagging feeling still remained in his gut that had been perceived, just not able to put a finger on it, but there was something not quite right with their first time meeting.

Sonders was radiant and oblivious to anything but his wife's beautiful face and the racing of his heart; everything seen now through eyes so clouded with love, he would not have noticed anything, even if it had hit him in the head, right between the eyes. With the wagon now loaded, all niceties were accomplished. Silas held Diablo for Caroleena to mount and, of course, with the aid of her new husband; Sonders now mounted upon Boston, and Silas driving the team pulled by the Percherons, Jericho and Whiskey. The three began their journey back to Oak Ridge Plantation—a fresh start for all; a new beginning, a new way of life for Silas, for Sonders, and indisputably, it most certainly would be for Caroleena.

*****

Arriving at last to Oak Ridge Plantation, Caroleena met Lucy; so impressed by Caroleena's beauty and stature; she matched everything Sonders had told her but detection of a sullen kind of attitude was upon Lady's face; her demeanor was belligerent. Lucy saw it, had seen it before on Mr. Frederick Barber's face, just before a whipping was about to happen out in the yard. Without a shadow of a doubt, that hostile leer was once again roosting on the land of Oak Ridge Plantation. But who could she tell? How would Lucy explain what she thought she had seen? Was it just a mirage, tiredness from a long, arduous trip from Charleston to Yemassee, and weariness from the horseback ride to Oak Ridge Plantation? Could it be the trip had taken its toll, and Caroleena was simply exhausted? Was experiencing all she had too overwhelming? And knowing what lay ahead for the rest of this day, simply had it been too much, all too exhausting for Caroleena? This had to be the answer. Lucy wanted it to be the answer.

Lucy took extra care to get Lady settled into her boudoir, adjacent to Mister's room. Fluffing pillows and encouraging Lady to lie down and rest, assuring her that the trip had to have been more exhausting than she may have realized, and that breakfast could wait, would wait. Caroleena did not object; she welcomed the privacy, the escape, and time.

Shutting the door to Lady's bedchamber, Lucy quickly sought out Silas, had to tell him what she had seen, couldn't keep this from her beloved, and maybe he wouldn't keep it from Sonders. Silas spoke with Lucy and their stories unraveled into similar observations. What they shared with one another were one and the same. But why? How could this be happening? What about Sonders? Does he deserve to be told, today of all days? Does Silas rip away the veil from Sonders' eyes? Or do they wait and let this play out for however long it may take until something else is noticed, to see if Caroleena is who she says she is?

Caroleena excused herself from going downstairs, telling Sonders she was simply too fatigued and needed to rest, all the while knowing that the evening's banquet was much more important than enjoying a breakfast together and only in front of the house slaves. Sonders, of course, understood, at least he told her that. Sonders was disappointed but knew her day had been a long one already, much longer than his day had been. So he gave her dismiss for the morning and afternoon to rejuvenate and refresh; he could not wait to introduce his bride to the rest of his world, now their world. And Caroleena could not wait to meet this new world, her next conquest.

Lucy was less than slightly disappointed to not be able to showcase her abilities of managing the Big House, for all the effort that had gone into the morning's breakfast, and countless days of preparation done to all the rooms. She had not even been given the pleasure of escorting Lady through each room and up to each level, describing the smallest of details, including a story here and there, hoping to show her lady that she would be in very competent hands, in Lucy's care.

Sonders ate a late breakfast in the large kitchen with Silas, a heavy look on his face, trying not to show it but too obvious to all there. Silas, in his usual nature, consoled and encouraged Sonders until the solemn look turned into a smile upon his face, bringing back to mind that this was his special day; Silas just could not bring himself to tell Sonders of his and Lucy's speculation now, something that he could not prove and hoped not to be able to do ever.

With breakfast now hours past, more serious attention would be given to the luscious meal and luxurious evening planned for the night ahead. It would be stupendous, memorable, the prelude to the night Sonders had dreamt of for weeks now. It had to be perfect. It would be perfect.

CHAPTER 10

The Banquet

Caroleena spent the afternoon reviewing in her mind, the plans long ago laid out in her mind's eye, plans had to be carried out perfectly, acting skills polished, and spoken words with just the right comments and compliments given about here and there, knowing all along everything said and done would have to deceive these partygoers. And her confidence was all she needed; she knew it could be pulled off, done too many times before in too many different circumstances. She was ready for whatever would happen; she would be ready for the challenge, of convincing everyone that she was the person she actually was not.

Ensuring that the last trunk she had forbidden Lucy to unpack, wouldn't even let her touch, was now stored and completely out of sight; and dressed in all the finery she owned, just for this occasion, Caroleena strolled the massive staircase, making her way to the bottom stairs. She looked perfect, walked perfectly, acted perfectly, and when Sonders greeted her at the bottom landing, she spoke perfectly and sealed their greeting with a tender kiss.

She had high expectations of the night. The appearance of the house, the ornamentation for the evening mattered, the house slaves on their best behavior, and guests who were simply unknown people to her now, but that would change. She would discover the one or two most valuable to her in fulfilling her plan and, of course, her expectations in her new husband, Sonders.

*****

Sonders reviewed the guest list once again and was pleased that everyone who should be here tonight to meet Caroleena had been invited. Beautiful handwritten invitations, sealed with an *O* from his insignia, stamped into indigo wax, hand-delivered under the oversight of Silas and specially selected servants, and all invited confirmed their attendance.

The Guest List
Announcing the Marriage of Sonders and Caroleena O'Ree

Sonders and Caroleena O'Ree of Graham Village
Oak Ridge Plantation

Harlan and Josephine Humphries of Spartanburg
Majestic Oaks Plantation

Walter and Callie Rutledge of Charleston
Rutledge Plantation

Reuben and Edyie Tison of Low Branch
Broad River Plantation

DeLacey and Tillie Rhodes of Colleton
Chechessee Plantation

Wesley and Mathilda Nelson of Williams Island
Euhaw Creek Plantation

Clayton and Louisa Willard of Harley Fork
Tupelo Plantation

Morris and Amelia Milton of Charleston
Wild Turkey Plantation

Marshall and Fannie Wigington of Zig Zag Branch
Great Swamp Plantation

Hiram and Estella Davis of Chatham
Lop Lolli Plantation

Neville and Lillian Wall of Yemassee
Mistletoe Grove Lane Plantation

Peter and Lucille Norris of Yemassee
Pheasant Run Plantation

Julian and Collette Simpson of New Orleans
Boulineau Plantation

Calvin and Rebecca Jane Benton of Graham Village
Sunnyside Track Plantation

Otto and Lydia Gillard of Altamaha Town
Magnolia Plantation

Grover and Etha Marion of Lawtonville
Barber, apothecary, and dry goods mercantile shop owner

Augustus and Miriam Allen of Yemassee
Tailor and restaurateur

Solomon and Bernice Simmons of Graham Village
Local sheriff and lawyer

Thaddeus and Mary Dunbar of Red Bluff
Banker and politician

Dr. Linnis and Jacqueline Merkel of Yemassee
Renowned Southern surgeon and local physician,
recent immigrants from Germany

Yosef and Frieda Eckstein of Graham Village
Jeweler, recent immigrants from Germany

Mordecai O'Ree of Graham Village
Communal preacher and father of the groom

*****

Glancing at how limited the decorations for the festivity were brought an immediate change of appearance in her face, even if only for a brief moment, of how disappointed she was, angry, almost furious, and Lucy and Silas had seen her, had caught the change in her face. They knew all their attempts in preparation for the festivity had fallen short of her lavish and set to high-standard tastes. They would brace for a possible scolding later but, for now, they would try even harder to please the new lady of the house. Caroleena quickly adjusted her scowled brow, just in time for Sonders to turn to ask her opinion. "Just lovely, simply beautiful, thank you" was all that she could muster.

*****

Guests soon began to arrive; carriages and horses and people milling around; slaves busy off-loading their passengers, hurriedly moving their curricle and two-horse team to the stable for safe harbor for the evening; making room for the next guests' arrival to Oak Ridge Plantation. Each guest, excitement building, anticipation brewing to meet the new mistress of Oak Ridge Plantation, the wife of Sonders Josiah O'Ree was imminent.

Sonders had joyously and enthusiastically extolled Caroleena's virtues to his many friends and neighboring plantation owners for the weeks since he last saw his bride. Their curiosity about this lady who had captured Sonders' heart was aroused, waiting had taunted their interest, but each now rewarded when this vision of loveliness entered into the grand foyer. Sauntering in on the arms of her new husband was the beautiful and enchanting Caroleena O'Ree.

Caroleena was introduced to each couple as they made their way into this grand home, the Big House, Oak Ridge Plantation. It was the envy of anyone who saw her and anyone lucky enough to be granted the invitation to go inside, privileged and set apart from the less fortunate not gathered.

Dinner was served. The Grand Dining Room was enormously sufficient to seat all the guests with not just the one eight-foot-long table set with all its fineries, but two additional tables brought in for just this occasion, and with plenty of room to spare. Guests all seated at their appointed place, along each side of each table, and with one more grand entrance to have their first meal together, announcements were made yet, again, welcoming the newly wedded couple, Sonders and Caroleena O'Ree. She loved the attention, the gazes upon her, and she knew they were looking at her, admiring, envying, jealous. Just as she had hoped.

With the banquet meal concluded, the honored couple and their guests retired to the Grand Ballroom, complete with crystal chandeliers and candles made to burn throughout the night, providing a well-lit room for all. Later this century, chandeliers would shed their light not from candles but from what would be called electricity, lighting up a glass bulb and illuminating a room with vibrant light but, for now, for tonight, the chandeliers in the Grand Ballroom would cast warm glows of light from the candles nestled in each nook constructed specifically into the arms of the growing layered tiers of each chandelier.

The house slaves had cooked all day, had served, and would eventually clean, but for now, the ones who were self-taught to play the fiddle and the flute and the banjo joined their celebration as performers, ensuring that the night would be filled with lively and spirited music, tunes for guests to enjoy, to kick their heels up to, drinking and playing and dancing and mingling and making merry. Oh, what a night to be remembered!

Caroleena required some fresh air, encouraging Sonders to stay and mingle with the guests; she would return directly to his side. She needed a moment alone, time to review the evening, the progress, among other things that she could do or correct to continue with her plan.

Once out on the portico, she breathed in the night air and noticed a gentleman out for a smoke from his pipe. Caroleena's eyes had found his at the long dinner table, and she couldn't help but notice his strong hands and handsome face. In this chance meeting, alone on a dark balcony, fate was shining brightly upon her. She could play naughty, even on her wedding night. Flirtation was her middle name. Playing with people's emotions at their expense was exhilarating and amusing. This could be her next conquest, after completing the Sonders O'Ree quest. The shadowed man knew she was newly married but decided to try his luck, to see where this experience might take him and with this rare beauty. He advanced toward her, eyes locked upon each other but, suddenly, alerted by noises nearby in the hedge, which distracted his progression; he left. Caroleena went back inside to rejoin Sonders. At that exact moment, Silas knew. He now had the proof. He had secretly followed Caroleena out onto the portico because of his own suspicions, now no longer doubts but real evidence.

Not long into this portion of the evening, Caroleena whispered to Sonders that she absolutely needed to retire to her bedchamber to regain some of her strength, her wit, and with the lowest, softest whisper, she reminded him of what the evening still had in store for them, together, alone.

Sonders announced that his bride would be adjourning for the night, after such an exhaustive day. Giving pleasantries to her guests and a warm lingering embrace to Sonders, Caroleena sashayed up the staircase and off into the night. No sooner had she left the ballroom, Silas presented Sonders with a note, a special guest and his wife had just arrived, delayed for poor weather along their travels, apologetic, disarrayed by rain and wind but still desperately trying to arrive for the banquet. Sonders welcomed his newly arrived friends in and introduced them to the crowd remaining. "Please meet Harlan and Josephine Humphries of Spartanburg, the new owners and planters of Majestic Oaks Plantation."

CHAPTER 11

Sealing the Deal

As the guests took their leave, and long-ago lit logs burned out their red-orange flames into smoldering cinders and embers, the long awaited evening's fire of passion was just to begin. It was time. That point of completing God's union of man and wife, the two becoming one flesh, no longer individuals but now one.

*****

He took her that night, consummated union from a vow made now a month ago, before God and their witnesses. Making love to Caroleena was the sweetest, most magical moment of his life; Sonders could not imagine anything quite so pure and innocent and as fulfilling and beautiful as his first time knowing this sort of union. Sonders knew Caroleena had experienced love before, but during her short lived marriage. He could only hope that this was just the beginning of endless, passionate nights that lay ahead for Mr. and Mrs. Sonders O'Ree, and that it had been just as special for Caroleena as it had been for him.

*****

She had anxiously awaited a month's passage of time to reach this day, to complete what had been set in motion in Charleston, to formally make their marriage a recognized and official union unto God, and before man. Most important to Caroleena was to keep a promise to herself of the plans she conceived years ago, to make everything right for herself, no one else, to move forward, regardless of what she may encounter.

Yet she had dreaded this day, she dreaded the night, the moment of giving herself to a man; not just any man this time but to Sonders, her newly wedded husband. This would complete their union as husband and wife. It had to be done. Caroleena knew all too well how to pretend, how to make anyone believe her, regardless of circumstance. And giving herself into the arms of lovemaking was just another cog in the wheel. Sonders would never know the difference.

This time was no more unique to Caroleena than telling the account of Majestic Oak Plantation's fate to fire or of the demise of the sniveling twin dolls (brats) to red-hot flames or, better yet, that she was a killer; no, not actually, just a nasty accident she had contrived and convinced so many of, most important Sonders. He had fallen into her trap, into her web of lies and deception.

Caroleena saw Sonders for who he was, a handsome man in every way: character, appearance, wealth. All these attributes combined spoke to the hidden yet decent side of Caroleena. Oh but for a brief moment in time, his charms made it easier to cloak her mind around their union. Her arms caressing his shoulders, his back supple to her fingertips, her body wrapped into his as one, giving in for a night of simple, fervent pleasure. Regardless of what she would take from Sonders, Caroleena always had her eye on the prize, the reward, a job well done. The plan would be completed, another step advancing her forward in conquering all she could amass to set things straight for all the wrongs that had been done to her.

Knowing to sigh at just the right moments, moving her body in rhythm with his assured Sonders of her commitment, her love, her passion, if only for that moment. Caroleena could endure this rare pleasure of physical ecstasy, both enjoying the union of what that night together would mean. She could never let Sonders see through her pretense, who she really was, what she was aiming for. Caroleena would do everything in her power to ensure that he would never know; and if making love with Sonders was the answer, then she would concede, fanning the flames of desire and, as often as necessary, she would yield.

CHAPTER 12

Secrets of Deception

First light came early, too early, and yet restless as the night had been, neither of them could wait for the darkness to be done. Much was on their minds. Troubled sleep, harrowing dreams, signs of betrayal, murmurings of evil, a dark spirit was lurking nearby. Silas knew it, Lucy knew it, and together they would prove it to their friend, their blood kin Sonders, but how?

Silas and Lucy had recognized the signs throughout the day and into the night, just yesterday, the day she had arrived. With their fears solidified by her promiscuous play on the portico, their pillow-talk plans began to take shape, how they would let Sonders know; plans were brewing. They didn't want to have to tell him, but they knew there was no other choice but to for his own good, for his sake. Sonders had to know Caroleena was up to no good.

*****

Caroleena slipped out of Sonders' arms, his warmth, his bed, and out into the quietness of the Big House at this early hour, early enough, hoping not to awaken him and returned to her own bedchamber. The deal was done, their bodies now made one; she was officially Mrs. Sonders Josiah O'Ree. Nothing nor no one could stop her now, especially Sonders.

It was expedient that she learn all she could about this place, about Sonders, about all that he possessed, all about Oak Ridge Plantation. Dressing quickly, she could ease outside and hopefully go unnoticed at least until midday, when a lady was to be expected up, rested, and dressed, and stirring about her home. But first, Caroleena needed to check one thing, the trunk, for peace of mind, one more time, just to be sure. Never make a mistake, don't overlook a thing. This philosophy had served her well in all the years of advancing her plan. And she was not about to make a mistake now. One error could ruin everything.

Pulling the trunk out from underneath heavy, tapestried bags and quilts that she had trusted for disguise, Caroleena worked quickly yet gently and quietly to open the lid. Peering inside gave Caroleena pleasure as she gazed upon the mass of wealth she had procured: Mother's bejeweled silver necklace with diamond pendant and her matching diamond bracelet and earrings; Father's gold and silver coins and bars, too many to stop to count; the deed of sale of Majestic Oaks Plantation; this top layer, just the beginning of what lay beneath. Her two escapades while studying in Philadelphia, and all at the unknown guise to Delia who simply thought she had lost some of her daddy's money. Deeds to properties, jewels and gems harvested from her brief marriage to Desmond Osgood were there. All just the beginning to her quest for a vast empire, domain, a place in society all to herself. Caroleena paused long enough, wondering when would enough be enough? How much more? When would her plan eventually come to an end? And yet, could it end? Did it have to end?

Closing the trunk, ensuring that the lid was secure and locked, she pushed it safely, deep into the back corner of the dark cedar-lined closet. Caroleena stood, smiled, and was satisfied. Tucking the key into a special place right where only she could find it, no one else could know, the corner of the silken pillowcase where she had laid her head, just yesterday, upon arriving at Oak Ridge Plantation, became the hiding place. Standing with fresh new hopes of being able to unlock the trunk again, and very soon, Caroleena would add more treasure, additional accomplishment, and with one more notch to mark into her proverbial belt of accomplishment, Caroleena exited the room to go investigate this next pawn in the game of chess, her life, a game that would eventually end but for now bringing endless possibilities and countless possessions her way.

Once outside, she knew the stroll out and across Oak Ridge Plantation would take the day. Not only did she want to take in its full beauty, she needed to measure just what she now had, had control of, had possession of that had now been sealed, for the day would eventually come when all of this, too, would be sold off bit by piece and section by parcel to become part of her past but yet to become a part of her future, her next accomplishment for her wealth and possessions and plan to grow and for her to succeed one more time.

*****

The typical morning at the Big House had begun. Lucy was up and about, seeing to the house slaves getting to their tasks; kneading and rolling out dough for the bread to bake; the grinder used each day, crushing coffee beans into miniscule grounds to be poured into countless cupsful of hot, black brew, and bringing an aroma unlike any other into the kitchen and beyond; collecting eggs from the hen house; the daily list goes on. But Lucy knew to be quick about her work as did Silas. Silas gathered and instructed his people to bring in firewood for each and every fireplace, warming each room in the Big House; removing chairs and the extra leaves of the grand dining room tables to store them away in the attic upstairs until needed again; and all this completed, preferably before Mister and Lady would be up and going.

*****

With morning chores over, and breakfast now complete, Sonders discovered the note Caroleena had left on his pillow.

My Darling,

I could not imagine waking you after the lovely night we shared. You were so peaceful. I have slipped out for a day of exploration of this beautiful place you have called home your entire life; and now, I am fortunate alongside you to call Oak Ridge Plantation my home. I cannot wait to be back in your arms and in your bed tonight, listening to your heartbeat, along with the sounds of silence of this house, to share our love together as one yet once again.

With all my love,
Caroleena.

(This long-ago written note was discovered by Aunt Ann de'Wees in an old family Bible that survived years of touch, time, and normal acidic degradation to paper that accumulates over time.)

Though Sonders desired to spend every waking moment with his new bride, he respected that she desired to discover her home, this new place where she would spend the rest of her life with him. And Sonders had his own pressing matter to attend to today, in the Village, procuring the special gift for Caroleena, something meant only for her.

*****

Lucy attended to Mister's room first, pulling the duvet and quilts and bedsheets from the four-poster highboy bed from a night of passion and sweat and sleep, remaking it with clean linens for this evening's frolic and sleep, ensuring ends of sheets were tucked in nice and neatly, enveloping the bed with its comfort and welcome once again. Opening up the heavy window curtains and slightly cracking the window to let in a bit of fresh air, Lucy passed through the doorway into Lady's boudoir. Of course, she had not slept here. She had been in Mister's room that night; the way it was supposed to be with new, young love.

Not having had time to straighten Lady's room from yesterday's arrival and nap until now, Lucy picked up her clothes left lying on the floor, from several wardrobe changes made throughout the day to meet the various needs of the Lady of the house and her day, pulling back the curtains to brighten the room, opening windows with plans to make fresh, particularly this time of year, when winter gives over to spring, and stuffy, stale air needing a renewed boost. The duvet had been rumpled slightly by Caroleena's rest yesterday while settling in. Nothing much was out of order here. The coverlet showed where her petite body had reclined, the pillow that she chose to rest her head. Straightening the bedding, and picking up the pillow to frump the down inside the silky pillowcase, Lucy heard a clang. Whatever this object was clinked heavily as it reached the oak floor below.

On knees, searching frantically, anxious about what might be found, Lucy ran her fingers underneath the oak bed, desperate to secure the object that had fallen from inside the pillowcase. Feeling the object and grabbing it with the tips of her fingers, she immediately knew what it was; a key, but to what? What had she stumbled upon?

Her mind rapidly rewound to the prior morning, when assisting Caroleena, aiding in putting her things away, suddenly and abruptly stopped by Caroleena from touching that last trunk, refusing her to touch it, to move it, or to assist in any way, form, or fashion. The rebuking look on Lady's face told Lucy that whatever was inside that trunk was off-limits, now and forever, the subject never to be brought up again. Reeling backward and cowling like a scolded dog and with no words spoken, Lucy knew there must be something inside that trunk that could change everything for Caroleena, for Sonders, and for them all.

Lucy knew Caroleena had gone out to stroll the grounds of this massive, expansive estate, and that she would be gone for quite a while. She quickly sought out Silas and brought him back into Lady's room. Lucy pulled the key from inside the top of her one-piece calico dress, inside the bodice slip that held her bosom tight. Frantically and quickly and desperately searching for the trunk, the two looked under the highboy bed, behind all the bedroom furnishings, and, lastly, the dressing screen that served as a privacy divider where Caroleena had disrobed and redressed just hours earlier. With nowhere else to look, they turned to the tall closet door. Opening it fully to allow for as much light to enter, they finally found the trunk nestled deep inside the closet in a darkened corner covered by Caroleena's bags and quilts. Pulling the trunk out into better light, Lucy handed the key to Silas. Silas slipped the key inside the lock, and turning it ever so cautiously, slowly, and yet deliberately, they both heard the click as the key opened the lock to this mysterious trunk that Caroleena had forbidden her to touch.

With both the hallway door and Mister's room door closed, Lucy listened intently for any sound of interruption that could possibly come. On crouched knees, and with quivering hands, Silas gently lifted the lid of the trunk; a muffled squeak of leather against wood was the only sound to be heard. With eyes widened, staring, amazed, their gazes were solely on the contents of…

What? What has Lady done? What is she up to? Where did all of this come from? What on earth is going on?

CHAPTER 13

The Cotton Field

Confident in herself, assured in her plans, poised for what this day may bring, Caroleena stepped off the last front porch step and out onto the acreage of her lands, her Oak Ridge Plantation. She had all day. She had the rest of her life, if this is what it would take, though that was a sure no; it would only be a matter of time before her next quest would come about. And that could be today.

Meandering along the various paths close by the Big House allowed Caroleena to appreciate all of this place's grandeur: the flower garden, where obviously the late winter, early spring flowers displayed for her and last night's gathering of guests, who were all amazed and stunned by such splendor this time of year, had been cut from and put on display; the vegetable garden down yet another path with winter salad greens of all kinds, and root vegetables such as radishes, cabbages, carrots, beets, and onions were still burrowed in the ground, ready to be plucked and cooked and eaten in some delicious tasty meal that Lucy would serve to all seated around her prepared table. Caroleena was amazed at the prospect of a bountiful harvest and very delighted in the complete order Sonders had the garden arranged in.

The most beautiful sight, just as she turned, brought her pause, had to stop, to admire, probably lingering for a bit too long was the view of the Big House in all of its glory. Splendid. Magnificent. And it was hers, all hers.

Attired in a full-skirted dress, plain and muted, soft-colored woolen fabric for this chillier time of year; a matching aproned front wrap with waist a tad shorter; her bosom padded by a soft muslin buffon neckerchief accentuating her elegant, delicate collarbone structure, and hips widened by the false rump of a ladies dress seen in this era of time, and with a cape draped over her shoulders, encasing her like a caterpillar cocooned, awaiting warmer springlike days to erupt from; Caroleena was set for her walk in these chilly temperatures of this early February day in the Low Country of South Carolina.

Caroleena was a true beauty, always kempt, always presentable, no matter the circumstance. Her blond locks dressed in a mass of loose curls and shrouded by an oversized, wide-brimmed flop hat, and smooth complexion pale, almost translucent with rosy-pink cheeks, crimson cherry lips, and sparkling blue eyes, she was a sight to behold. Caroleena had it all, her looks, her trunk of a life's possessions, and now her continued plan to fulfill it all.

Pondering and contemplating everything, Caroleena continued with her walk; the midmorning sun now bathing down more of its warmth and rays to illuminate and brighten her day. She admired the way the sun had come up in the morning sky, illuminating the gardens and this beautiful, unique estate. Caroleena looked forward to enjoying this same vision of loveliness more than once in the coming days, weeks at most.

Her steps took her past a gathered group of male slaves totally involved in plowing with a team of oxen, tilling the sandy soil into large gray-brown mounds for planting of some upcoming crop.

Wandering farther into the plantation, another group of slave women were tending to very young children, all the while snapping beans; some washing clothes in a large cast-iron pot placed strategically over a fire to bring the water to a boil for proper cleansing. Others were cleaning freshly gathered potatoes and root vegetables recently pulled from the garden.

Further into her stroll, she came upon the cotton field where long rows of cotton seeds were being hand-fed into each hole dug specifically for that plant to grow up in; and though planting cotton seed this time of year was a bit premature, everyone around predicted an early spring to the region. The seed would be nurtured into a cotton-producing plant that would soon benefit Mister as well as all of the slaves on this plantation, just as the cotton harvest just recently passed was bumper to Oak Ridge Plantation.

Slaves were all along this part of the cotton field; no one near the other, and each one working hard with the day just beginning. One slave, a female slave, seemed to be struggling over something; Caroleena drew closer, her curiosity always ahead of her.

*****

Her morning came a little too soon as the night's telling was that today was going to be the day that her baby would be born. Leona was heavy with child. And her husband, Amos, was equally concerned; but work was inevitable for them both. Amos would be at work in an entirely different part of the cotton field today. They never saw each other from dawn to dusk. Working field slaves tolerated a six-day workweek, very little rest in each day, but thank the Lord for Sundays. Couldn't this child wait until Sunday? Wouldn't he wait just a few more days?

With a kiss on the head, Amos reluctantly left Leona and walked off and out to his place in the field to work. Leona mustered her strength and resolve to get up and get at it. On this particular Thursday, Leona knew that she was in the process of giving birth. Thanking the Lord for a sunny, warm day—not frigidly cold or rainy as it could have been; at least this was in her favor. Now fully positioned into her place in the field, Leona went to work, bending down, poking holes into the mounds of soil waiting for their seed to go in, all the while waiting for her ripe seed to burst forth.

As the morning went on, she knew this baby was about to drop. Groans, pains, cries out to the Lord Jesus to help her; Leona was giving birth to this baby. It was time. It would drop.

*****

It was unusual to see the lady of any plantation walking about this time of day and yet all alone. But here was Caroleena, walking the perimeter of the section of field that Leona worked. As Caroleena was gazing out over her newly acquired estate and, in particular, this cotton field, she neared the scene. She had heard groaning and moaning, sounds that she had not heard since the twin brats were preparing to make their entrance into this world, before taking Mother away from her.

Seeming to take the longest of time watching this woman, heaving, writhing, whimpering, clutching her belly, finally flopping down onto the ground, knees agape, hands down between her legs, and with one last and loud groan, the baby burst forth in its own river of waters from inside her, the slave woman Leona had brought forth life. And with that, Caroleena had witnessed her first birth.

The baby was covered in wetness and blood as Leona held the child, with it making its first mewing sounds as soft as a kitten but yet as fierce as a lion. Was it seeing an actual birth or hearing a baby's first cries? Was it a moment of delirium that caused her to do what she did next? Caroleena would never know.

In a fleeting moment of maternal goodness and trying to justify her yearnings, Caroleena envisioned this baby as hers. Why, she had witnessed it coming into this world as if it was her own. This was a child whom she could have but refused at the arms of Desmond Osgood. Or maybe, just maybe, she could have been there for her sisters and mothered the twin brats. It didn't take long for her to return to herself, her contriving and wicked senses, and realized she couldn't take a Black baby back to the Big House and into Sonders' life. She would never want his children either.

Caroleena did not know what was coming over her, except that she could later explain the reason of having a moment of rationality, where she found the better side of herself. She wanted this baby, wanted to hold this baby, wanted to be this baby's mother. And in a blink of an eye, Caroleena moved over beside Leona, tearing off her own cream-colored, lacy apron that was simply tied at the back, snatched the baby with umbilical cord still attached, yanked it from this woman's body and her clutched arms. She wrapped and swaddled the baby tightly to her own breast, blood and wetness soaking in through her own cape and dress. Holding the baby away from his mother, Caroleena sternly reprimanded the slave woman. Behind gritted teeth and leering eyes, Caroleena barked that she had better not say a word to anyone or else there would be a price to pay. Caroleena scuttled quickly away, leaving this slave woman and this cotton field, swaddling the baby, hoping no one had seen or would have noticed.

What Caroleena did not know, and would have cared even less about had she known, was that her action of snatching the baby with the umbilical cord still attached had caused Leona to retain the placenta within her body. Because of the traumatic way this had been handled, the cord being ripped away from the placenta, it did not fully deliver. Shortly after she gave birth, Leona began to hemorrhage, and with no one nearby to hear her weakened cries for help, Leona bled out and soon thereafter died, right there where she had given birth, and would not even be discovered until after dark later that night.

What had she done? This was all wrong. There was no rhyme or reason as to why she really did it. Her mind wouldn't let her make sense of it. And as she ran, Caroleena knew that she had to make it go away. But how? Where?

And then she stopped and listened. And for a brief moment, and from a distant calling, Caroleena heard the waters. It was nearby. Black Mingo. The water was her answer. The water would be this baby's refuge, and the water would be her salvation from this mess.

CHAPTER 14

River's Edge

Justifying came heavy to her mind. Why, this was just a small piece of her new empire, of her wealth, her love of things; it just happened so fast. She deserved this, whatever she wanted, whatever life had to offer. That is what the years had taught her.

She had come upon this scene. It wasn't her fault, it was the slave woman's doing; she made it look so complete, to be a woman, to do what a woman was made to do, to make and have babies, so why not her? She had to have this wee child for her very own. That's why she had grabbed the baby; yet in her very next breath, she understood that she couldn't keep the infant, a very Black baby. She had only wed and consummated her union with Sonders just the night prior to. How could she hide it? And what would Sonders think? What would he say? What would anyone think of her? She couldn't afford to have this mar on her reputation or to interfere with her plans. She had no explanation, had no answer. What had she been thinking?

Caroleena did not want a baby. She did not have any mothering instincts. Wrapped tightly in her apron, now drenched in birthing fluids, the baby looked almost White, covered in the vernix caseosa. The medical term *vernix caseosa* would first be recognized in the dictionary of medical sciences in 1846, being described as the naturally occurring white, creamy-looking substance coating the baby while inside its mother, providing protection to its skin. Could she get away with it?

Her mind was going back and forth as a ball bouncing to and fro, trying to rationalize what she had done. Yet knowing all along what the answer was, she knew the answer was no. Caroleena fled, hurriedly scampering down toward the bank. As she neared, Black Mingo looked as though it was holding its arms out to take this newborn life away from Caroleena, to swaddle it for her. Caroleena could not go back. She could not simply give this child back to the slave woman. She would tell someone. And then, what would Sonders think? She had to make this poor decision vanish, to go away, this thing that was now whimpering and crying and coughing and needing its mother, not Caroleena. She had nothing to offer this baby.

Shucking off the soaked and ruined apron from around this baby, Caroleena dropped it as she quickly passed near one of Uncle Henry's long outstretched arms; this child no longer needed a covering for protection, a blanket for warmth. She proceeded toward the water. Approaching the river's edge, Caroleena kicked off her low-heeled, leather-laced shoes; and now standing in stocking feet, Caroleena waded out into ankle-deep water. Staring at this tiny human, all red and black and white and covered in dried blood and birth matter, Caroleena knew there was only one answer, and that was to end this life she had stolen so that she could continue with her own.

Holding the shivering infant just inches above the cold running waters, knowing that it would not take long to end this bad situation that she brought on herself, Caroleena hesitated one more time. She had to proceed. She had to do away with it, had to erase this from any possible memory other than her own. The chilly morning air and the cold waters of Black Mingo would soon take over; they would do the job for her, they would be in control. And then the last chapter of this not-well-written page of her life would come to an end. Watching life squirm, peering into this baby's eyes, Caroleena slowly submerged the body, pushing a life down into an endless sea of running waters; of Black Mingo's winter-cold rushing waters.

*****

What was not obvious to anyone in that moment was that Silas had gone down to Uncle Henry, just minutes earlier, just after he and Lucy had made their discovery, had to go out and think, to ponder what had been found and what it could mean. How was he to tell his brother, Sonders, the person he loved most in this world?

Sitting eight to ten feet up or so, out on one of Uncle Henry's strongest and biggest limbs, Silas held a burlap bag just so, ready and waiting to catch the possum that he had been tracking for weeks now, one of the biggest he had ever seen. And it would make for a fine stew for sure. After climbing up and onto one of Uncle Henry's moss-covered limbs, Silas sat, watching, waiting, and wondering when to make his move. The possum showed, appeared almost out of nowhere, and it was moving out from the edge of the limb, coming closer toward Uncle Henry's trunk, right where Silas sat. The possum crawled closer, right up to the open end of the burlap bag. He must have been blind to have not seen the bag or Silas.

Just as Silas was about to snap the bag around that ole possum's neck, a sound caught his ear, a sound that he had never heard before. He looked around, down toward the river's edge, still scanning, and on up a ways along the bank, there was Caroleena, walking into the water; in stocking feet; and holding a… What?

It was then and there that he saw a tiny newborn infant in Caroleena's outstretched arms, hands trembling, body shaking. Completely unable to utter a sound, Silas was seized by convulsive retching upon witnessing this shocking act unfolding before his eyes. He was even unable to muster a scream or even the slightest whimper to try to stop her. Silas could only watch as Caroleena plunged that poor thing to its death in the cold waters, raging and running rapidly, deep into Black Mingo, that old Coosaw River.

CHAPTER 15

The Gift

Sonders had thought about doing this since the day he said I do. Planned it out just so and just for her. Aunt Emma would be so proud of him and be so pleased that her heirloom would be passed on, worn, cherished, and treasured. If only she were here to know about his surprise for her, to help him make some decisions, too, about how to bring perfection out of something already so beautiful. His own plans, with the help and opinions of Lucy, well, they were more than sufficient.

Caroleena was already up and gone from the Big House when Sonders began to stir. He was a bit relieved when Caroleena told him she wanted to roam the grounds this day and preferably alone, to take it all in, felt like having him along might make her too emotional, considering all that Sonders had described and detailed about Oak Ridge Plantation. Her note had assured Sonders that he had the liberty of the day to do as he pleased, and this pleased him more than he could put into words.

Sitting up tall and high in the well-worn saddle that his backside had become quite accustomed to over the years, and with reigns in hand, Sonders was off on his way. Riding Boston had been a pleasure he had enjoyed for many years, and today, it was just him and his horse, both settled in and ready for the day. Boston knew the way into the Village. So with very little guidance, Sonders was able to take in the brisk morning air and the scenery of this late winter morning here in the Low Country as the horse trotted toward the Village. This was just what Sonders needed, time to reflect on the last month of how his life had so drastically changed; meeting her had changed everything, and it was so very good. His thoughts brought warmth and a comforting feeling to him completely, mind, body, and soul. Nothing could spoil this day.

Sonders was pleased that the newly arrived family to Graham Village, Mr. and Mrs. Yosef and Frieda Eckstein, had accepted the invitation to dinner and to meet his lovely bride. What seemed like days ago was only just last night; and both he and Caroleena had enjoyed the pleasure of getting to know the Ecksteins, Yosef and Frieda, more personally.

The Ecksteins had recently immigrated to this new land from Germany, after hearing about endless opportunities in trade, export and, not to mention, the tremendous growing wealth that the South afforded to those willing to try their luck here. It was considered a land overflowing with milk and honey or so some of the wealthier plantation planters liked to say, comparing it to the promised land. Yosef was a self-taught jeweler with most of his attained accomplishment during his apprenticeship while in Paris, working in a French jewelry house known for diamond masterpieces in adornment for the ladies and for the finer established gentlemen of that time.

Yosef hoped to share his fine quality jewelry, coming with a fine price, with the Southern planters, and with being so close to Charleston, Savannah, and both ports, and the promise that this particular region of the South would one day be a gold mine; Yosef was convinced his decision was sound.

Not long after returning from Charleston and having wed the lovely Caroleena, Sonders knew he wanted to present her with something very special, once she arrived to Oak Ridge Plantation. He recalled the inherited jewelry box that Emma had kept. With great intent, he had found the bin that he had relocated to the attic of the Big House, and safely stored inside was Emma's jewelry box.

Sonders perused the contents, finding the perfect piece. A marvelous cameo and necklace, Emma O'Ree's, an heirloom handed down from several generations, from her grandmother to her mother and then to her where the handing down ended. Emma had treasured the cameo. Sonders recalled Emma wearing it for very special occasions, remembered seeing it around Emma's neck that last Christmas before she and Barnabas died. It was stunning then, and it was stunning now. Sonders could now imagine the necklace adorning Caroleena's delicate, slender, and feminine neck. This would be the crown jewel for her. This was the piece, the perfect gift to present to his bride, an exquisite cameo, which was apropos for the lovely Lady of Oak Ridge Plantation.

Sonders entered Yosef's Jewelers, the shop at the end of the Village, and was greeted by Frieda with a curtsy and hearty hello. Yosef entered from behind a long, burgundy curtain, meant to shield a prospective buyer from his workshop area. Immediately disappearing behind the curtain and returning within minutes, Yosef held out the box. Sonders opened the lid and gazed at the cameo. Yosef had remade the cameo into a piece lovelier than one could imagine, and Sonders was more than pleased.

With monies exchanged and appreciation given, more than once, Sonders and Yosef conversed as Frieda completed the purchase by adding pink rosebud paper wrapping and adorning the box with a piece of matching ribbon. Yosef motioned for Sonders to join him outside for a puff of the pipe, to smoke some of his special tobacco recently purchased while traveling through Spartanburg, where he purchased diamonds and other gems for his jewelry-making business.

More pleasantries exchanged, and relighting and puffing their pipes, Yosef thanked Sonders again for the lovely evening he and Frieda had enjoyed the night before. It was good to be welcomed and introduced to his many friends and neighbors. Good future business the way Yosef saw it.

Smoke wafted, and their puffing and relighting their pipes continued, making for light, easy conversation. Yosef spoke of his travels through upstate South Carolina; such a beauty that part of this region was, and his time while in Spartanburg, well, what an extraordinary town it was; the experience there unforgettable. And then last night, what a coincidence and surprise when being introduced to Harlan and Josephine Humphries, well, he had made their acquaintance before.

Yosef went on to say that he had met the Humphries shortly after their purchase of Majestic Oaks Plantation and thought them to be fine, upstanding society. And in their short time together last evening, Yosef thought he had understood Harlan to mention that they had bought the estate from a Caroleena Lumford Osgood. Yosef had not thought much more of this but simply thought it a coincidence of the first name of Caroleena, not a common name and yet a name now associated with two plantations: Majestic Oaks Plantation and Oak Ridge Plantation.

Sonders stared past Yosef, trying to remain focused on the rest of what he was saying; but as impossible as that was, Sonders heard something that didn't mesh with the way he had understood things, things Caroleena said about her upbringing, where she was from, school, marriage, losing everything, right up until the time he had met her, just a month ago. His mind was reeling. He felt a bit dizzy. Sonders excused himself, taking the package, thanking Frieda and Yosef once again, and somehow managed to mount Boston. Sonders snapped the reins on Boston's hind quarters, alerting him that it was time to go and go quickly.

The ride home back to Oak Ridge Plantation was a blur. Nothing like the ride into the Village. His mind was skewed, foggy, confused. What exactly had he just heard? His heart was telling him one thing, but his mind and all reason was screaming, *Caroleena, what have you done?*

CHAPTER 16

A Fisherman's Tell

Silas could not wrap his mind around what he had just seen. Shock had held him back, keeping him quiet and as inconspicuous as a titmouse, and fear of approaching her because of his place in life, and who he was—a slave—made him bite his tongue. He had no idea what this woman would have done had he intervened, but that would not prevent him from telling his master, his brother, Sonders. Never.

Gagging and shaking beyond control, Silas waited until she was gone, out of sight, obviously to change her clothing due to the sight that she was covered in blood. Climbing down from Uncle Henry's arms, Silas slipped through a thick hedge of azalea bushes and back up to the Big House using a different path to attempt to gather himself. His body was wet from sweat by the time he reached his quarters; not just from the sprint he had made from Black Mingo to his bed, but he took extra precaution so as to not be seen or heard by this person, this killer, or whoever she was.

Pacing the floor, he contemplated telling Lucy, but it wasn't the right time for that yet. Lucy would know all too soon. Silas knew that he would tell his brother today; it had to be today, and as soon as he returned from the Village, he would. A few plans laid out in his thoughts of what he needed to tell Sonders were now in order; from the first to the last of what he had seen, and with his own eyes, from this woman since her arrival at the train station, just two mornings earlier. It was settled; as soon as Sonders returned, he would tell him. And what better way than to grab a fishing pole and take him down to Black Mingo, their spot, a place where they could talk about anything, the perfect place for him to disclose everything. Silas would tell Sonders the whole lot of Caroleena's actions, and this was going to turn his world upside down.

*****

Letting Boston run hard at it, riding wildly and feeling out of control, Sonders' mind was racing. What Yosef had disclosed, no harm meant, was all needing to be said. What was the ditty about the purchase of Majestic Oaks Plantation to the Humphries and from whom had Yosef said? Did he hear him correctly? Did he say Caroleena Lumford Osgood? And for the first time since meeting this lovely creature, Sonders experienced a rush of concern, a hair of conflict and suspicion battled through his mind. This was not what Caroleena had told him. This could not be the Caroleena he knew.

Boston had trotted into town earlier that morning. Now Sonders had him in a full on gallop. He needed to get home, to face what he dreaded. Knowing the way all too well, Boston turned just where he had so many times, off the main road from the Village, and toward the Big House. Sonders felt out of control. His mind was considering terrible things, but she would make this all go away; she would have the answers to his muddied questions, and she would need to address them and soon.

Coming into view now was the Big House; and Sonders, recognizing the same structural face of greeting that was always on display by this opulent home, he gained assurance from the house's safe harbor, that somehow everything was going to be all right, even if it would be but for a brief moment of certainty. Standing at the bottom of the wraparound porch and front steps was Silas, waiting for his brother, just as he always was, always there waiting patiently but now anxiously for his brother, Sonders, to return home. Silas had his own list of fears to share. No longer just suspicions, now provable and irrevocable facts; and they seemed to keep mounting with each passing hour.

Seeing the fishing pole in Silas's hand quickly took Sonders to a place of peace and tranquility in his mind, always a good place. He knew Silas must have sensed that he needed this today, above all days. Silas took Boston's reins to lead him to the stable while Sonders changed into more suitable clothing for their adventure and to put the gift deliberately away and out of sight, in a place that no one could find it.

The walk was silent. The path was leading. Roscoe and Jasper licking at their heels to go on an adventure as they always were ready to go. In their silence, Sonders knew that he had to tell Silas what he had heard, and he sensed that

Silas in turn needed to tell him something too. Could it be that he had already noticed something about Caroleena too? Maybe even seen something? Disturbed thoughts were taking control of his being. Silas could see the troubled look on Sonders face, and he detected the same with him. Silas needed to tell Sonders everything that he now knew. No longer were they simply doubts or suspicions. And it didn't feel good knowing that he had to tell his brother things that would break his heart and alarm him beyond shock. This day was not going to be a good day in many ways.

Uncle Henry's welcoming arms were in sight, but their canine companions were leading them in a different direction than where the brothers preferred to set up, their secret fishing spot, underneath a sturdy, moss-covered limb of Uncle Henry's that stretched out just a bit over the running waters of Black Mingo. The dogs were running now, barking and howling. They were tracking. They were on the hunt. Sonders and Silas followed with a quickened pace but knew their boys wouldn't go too far; those dogs knew all too well how to get home if they went on a day's tangent, off and away from their master.

Approaching where Roscoe and Jasper had stopped; still growling but stopped now from tracking their prey, Sonders and Silas stopped abruptly in their tracks. Both Roscoe and Jasper had a piece of an edge of tinged cloth in their mouths, wrestling over who was going to win the prize. The dogs had tracked the scent of a bloodied, much-discolored lady's apron. That's what it was. Complete with lace and apron strings for tying, and blood, lots of varied tones of red blood soaked through and through this delicate and dainty cloth apron, right where it had been dropped, just hours earlier.

Sonders pulled Jasper away as Silas worked to wrangle the cloth from Roscoe's gritted teeth. They both knew they'd done good, really good. But both dogs weren't finished yet. Pulling and yanking to get away, they were on the hunt for something more. Intent on following Roscoe and Jasper, they moved closer to the bank of Black Mingo's waters. And just a few steps away from their secret fishing hole, they were jolted to stop. They both saw it at the same time. A tiny, completely formed body. It was a newborn baby.

Somehow, the unattached end of the umbilical cord had become ensnared in some of Uncle Henry's Spanish moss and limb twigs and shoots that dipped down into Black Mingo's waters. And now wrapped and entangled in moss and muck, this tiny baby seemed sheltered in the moss, almost like Uncle Henry was trying to cradle it, to protect it, but it was too late.

The body had obviously not been in Black Mingo's cold waters for very long. Though air in its tiny lungs had been replaced with cold, murky water, the infant's skin had wrinkled only slightly; vernix caseosa still provided some protection as if this baby were still in utero, still inside its mother, waiting for life to begin. The body not yet bloated from much decomposition as Black Mingo's colder waters had almost acted as an insulator to the body, preventing bacteria in the gut and chest from forming too fast that would eventually produce enough gas to make the body float. This baby was floating now because it had been ensnared and kept by Uncle Henry; the waters ever pulling to free it, but Uncle Henry was holding tight. He would not let go.

No sooner had this little one taken its first breath than the water replaced its life-giving lungs with fluid, instead of air. This poor little soul. Sonders' first thought was who would have done this but, within minutes, his sad forlorn face took a turn to anger, disgust, and contortion as he began to put two and two together. The apron, this baby's body; he turned to Silas for answers. Silas hung his head for a brief moment of shame and disgust in himself for not doing something to help rescue this newborn baby. Then his eyes locked on Sonders. "It was Caroleena, my brother."

Silas continued with all the things he had discovered about this evil yet alluring creature as they shrouded the body best they could in the bloodied apron and started their walk back to the Big House. His daunting discoveries to have to tell him shook Silas to his core and Sonders as well. Once Silas completed his list of findings—the gentleman on the portico at the banquet, the trunk of possessions in her closet, and now witnessing her drown this poor baby; it was Sonders' turn to tell Silas what Yosef had divulged. It was Caroleena Lumford Osgood who owned Majestic Oaks Plantation and, through her lies and deceit, had tricked Sonders into believing her to be someone else. These things all now disclosed and discovered and believed about his beloved Caroleena.

Silas and Sonders had both been one another's lifetime confidants so it took no convincing by Silas for Sonders to see and believe that this had to be dealt with and soon.

CHAPTER 17

A Restless Night

The night was dark and yet was as enchanting as a sweet dream. A thick gloom held heavy in the shadows of the darkness and all throughout the Big House. Listening close enough, one could hear the house breathing; the ticking of the one-hundred-year-old grandfather clock as his pendulum swung back and forth, and even the heartbeats of both Caroleena and Sonders that had been merged together, were now being torn apart.

Evening's light was already spent, and the supper together had been more than quiet, predominantly silent, except for the one remark of Caroleena, complaining of a headache, possibly from having spent too long outside that day; the cooler late winter's air must have taken its toll. She had lost all track of time while strolling along the estate paths and simply overexerted herself, caught up in watching the slaves working and letting the day get ahead of itself had affected her, giving her this present difficulty; at least this is how she explained it to Sonders.

No other exchange was shared between the two. As they both nibbled from their plates, Sonders and Caroleena both realized that things were awry and may never be corrected. Silas and Lucy watched from their waiting positions, both so wanting to push forward the hands of time and wishing this all away.

Regardless, Caroleena felt it best to sleep in her own bed this evening. And Sonders had no qualms with her suggestion, nodding his head in complete agreement. The fact of the matter was this separation brought relief to his mind and an almost contentment to his heart thinking about not having to lie with his wife; even should a possible romantic twinge arouse within him; something that had whetted his being with fire and desire that he had so longed for just the night before. How just twenty-four hours had literally changed everything for everyone.

*****

Amos was completely worried now that his day's work was over, and Leona was nowhere to be found. Amos remembered his last glance of Leona this morning as she was clutching her belly and ready to drop their first child. He knew it best to seek out the help of his Planter and friend; they would know how to help. A rap at the door alerted Lucy to find Amos shaking and shivering, and with a fearful, desperate look on his face, she immediately knew who Amos had come to see. Not knowing exactly where Leona would have been working that particular day in the fields, Amos had already been searching to no avail and now needed the guidance of Silas and Sonders.

With lanterns held high, and Roscoe and Jasper's noses peeled on to the scent of Leona, it didn't take very long to find her lifeless, cold body laid out, sprawled on the open ground, body angled to one side, knees flopped over, hands dug into the dirty sandy soil, now clogging the tips of her fingernails; obviously indicating that Leona had tried to find stability to assist her rise, only to fall from her extremely weakened condition, there she lay. A tremendous amount of blood was all around Leona, at least that which had not soaked into her simple cloth dress or into the ground. It was clear she had given birth. Amos crouched down to his beloved Leona, sobbing with moaning and utterances unidentifiable to the men standing with him, lifting her lifeless body to his chest, and holding tight to the love of his soul; Amos knew he was losing most of his heart in an instant of time. What wicked and immoral creature could have done this? And why to his precious Leona? Silas and Sonders knew the answers to his pleadings, and his questions would be answered and very soon.

The newborn had been taken from her; whether before she died or afterward, they may never know that but, for now, the very least they could do and would do was to reunite the two and put to rest mother and baby, bury them together, just as they had been at the start of this day, together forever.

With Oak Ridge Plantation being a very large estate, the O'Ree family had long ago set aside a graveyard dedicated as an everlasting resting place for the souls who had been freed from slavery and placed into death's hands for the here and after and into eternity. And as Sonders held the lantern for Silas and Amos to see, together they dug a deep-enough grave to hold both bodies, his beloved Leona and the baby whom Amos had never held until now. He placed his son into Leona's arms, lovingly and carefully, appearing as though he didn't want to wake either of them. Let them rest together from here to eternity. Silas helped cover them both with an old but well-kept quilt that Sonders so graciously provided for their burial. As the three men bowed their heads, Amos began to shovel dirt into the grave, onto his beloved wife and little boy. Sonders spoke these words of comfort, hope, and promise: "Fear thou not; for I am with thee: be not dismayed; for I am thy God: I will strengthen thee; yea, I will help thee; yea, I will uphold thee with the right hand of my righteousness" (Isaiah 41:10 KJV).

Knowing he needed to console Amos, Silas saw him back to his small house situated not far from the Big House. Amos and Leona had enjoyed this privilege of being close to the Planter's house with fortune of having a better-built structure and with a bricked chimney to their fireplace, allowing for more heat to be retained inside. Now Amos would spend his time there, alone, and with just his memories of what it had once been, their home.

*****

Sufficiently pleased, though a little shaken by the mar that had occurred earlier, well aware that she had let her guard down a little too much, allowing for an external, unexpected incident to affect her so, a minor setback as she saw it; but that had all been discretely taken care of, so not to worry, she assured herself. This day had brought about her plans nicely, though more accelerated than she had thought they would be, just two days into her journey here on Oak Ridge Plantation.

With a bit more intensity now, Caroleena had been forced to move the pawn in her mind's plan forward. But it would work. She would see to that. Caroleena had to keep all the important factors in place of advancing her plan, to gain all that she could and while she could, all the while keeping in mind her age, her mental and physical well-being, reputation, and goals yet to attain. The more pressing objective—taking over Oak Ridge Plantation; making it hers, no longer his, not theirs together, but hers, completely and legally hers.

As the hours passed, barely moving her petite body from the place she first lay down, the outline of tomorrow took on a flawless shape, one that pleased her well. Sleep came easily to her invigorated mind, once she ran through the course of the day's plot one more time. "Perfect," she said aloud. This is the best laid-out strategy of them all. Tomorrow night this time, she would no longer just be Mrs. Sonders Josiah O'Ree; she would be the pitied and consoled Mrs. Caroleena Lumford Osgood O'Ree, widow of the late Sonders J. O'Ree.

*****

All these pieces to this horrific puzzle were spinning uncontrollably in his thoughts. This was mind-boggling. But the final piece was missing. And that would fit perfectly once put into its proper place tomorrow, when Sonders would complete his own scheme of removing evil from Oak Ridge Plantation; he saw no other way out.

As Sonders saw it, evil had dwelled here for too long a stint already. It was during a time when Mr. Frederick

Barber had worked the estate as head slave captain, when Uncle Barnabas O'Ree was the Planter of Oak Ridge Plantation. From stories all too familiar to Sonders, he recalled it a horrifying time where rule was by an iron fist, and a select few souls suffered immensely under the charge of Barber's tenure. That evil had been expelled by Barnabas not so long ago. And come hell or high water, this evil would be banished, and by a different set of O'Ree's hands, by those of Sonders O'Ree.

Surrounded by a haunting silence and just his own thoughts now, Sonders tried to rationalize his decision. Silas had agreed. But at what cost? Could he proceed with plans of their own? Or should he simply rise and go confront her now?

Pulling back the covers, stockinged feet already on the floor, never-known-before thoughts and feelings moved him forward, toward her door, Sonders mumbled to himself that it was going to be a gamble either way, and he knew it. But he also was well aware beyond a shadow of a doubt that it had to be done. Sonders had to do away with this evil that had come to roost at Oak Ridge Plantation and into his life, into too many lives. Enough would be enough.

Gathering himself, Sonders let go of the cold brass handle of the doorknob of Lady's boudoir and turned back to his own bed. Sonders heard himself mutter, "It would be handled by tomorrow, and it would all start at first light."

Sonders' heart was no longer flamed by the fires of passion and love and all things pure and good. His thoughts now were stoked by the fire of reality, pure disbelief of it all, the complete brokenness of trust, and all of it, all because of her, a complete lie.

Restless, no sleep would come to ease his mind. Lying underneath the warm coverlet and winter quilt, he recognized that this was his responsibility as Planter to right this ship. But his mind was muddied with so many decisions to make and actions to take, especially when he lingered on the piece of him doing the unthinkable, something that he would have never fathomed himself doing, and that was to take life from someone, to be the hands of God.

The reality of the deception and evil this woman had brought here to Oak Ridge Plantation and into his world, could no longer grow its roots here or any deeper than they had already taken hold of. Nor would he allow giving further life to the wickedness in persona of Caroleena Lumford Osgood O'Ree. With nerves electrified, he knew there was no turning back now. Sonders would not falter with his plan, his plot to destroy evil, his newly wedded bride, Caroleena.

Morning came at last, and Sonders quickly found Silas, disclosing his full-on design for the day ahead. Silas did not wince, did not flinch, did not ever second-guess all that he had just heard. He had always been there for Sonders, and today would be no different. With some trepidation about what would soon follow, the two blood brothers plodded off to the kitchen to make ready the first part of their plan.

CHAPTER 18

The Guise of Sustenance

In the early hours of this morning, the typically busy kitchen was now empty and quiet, except for Lucy, who was fully involved in making up a breakfast hamper for the outing that Mister and Lady would be shortly taking, that is if the cold late winter rain would ever stop falling.

The fires had not been stoked nor were the two matching ivy-patterned crocks that were usually filled with frothy milk gravy and fluffy fresh scrambled eggs ready to be set on the table; they remained empty. There was enough bread from last night's barely eaten supper that Lucy thought it sufficient for the day's requirements on Oak Ridge Plantation. She would not take the time to bake additional loaves, though the warmth from the hearth and fireplace would be missed on such a day as this. Today was an odd day for sure. Nothing like usual at all.

The Big House kitchen, of course, was not connected to the main house. Over a hundred years ago, when Allister O'Ree had this estate built, it was with purpose that the kitchen was just around back and secluded out of sight from the Planter's home and their view, had to keep the opulence and presentation of Oak Ridge Plantation as close to perfect as possible; and he had succeeded. Being separated would also keep any out of control fire in the kitchen from damaging anything beyond its walls; though this time of year, any additional heat would have been welcomed. Lucy couldn't tell if she was rubbing her hands together for the friction to bring warmth to her cold, chilly fingers or if she was wringing her hands from nerves and anxieties that her gut was obviously reminding her of; both reasons were probably correct.

Lucy had sensed the heavy tension in the air and throughout all the passageways of the Big House last night; probably because she knew Silas was with Sonders, telling him everything, ridding himself of too many of that woman's evil secrets, and yet knowing the heavy burden he was placing on Sonders' shoulders from hearing the truth about pure immorality that had come to be on Oak Ridge Plantation. This truth would break his mind and cut deep into his heart. It had to be this way. Silas had no other choice.

Sonders and Silas met Lucy in the kitchen; no one was speaking a word—they didn't have to. The air was as solemn as the funeral for Leona and her baby boy, just the night before; and the tension could be cut in half with a sharp butcher's knife, had they tried. There was no turning back now. It had begun.

Lucy would find herself uttering brief prayers before the Lord throughout the morning, knowing what her dear husband and Mister would be facing, having to carry out, and what the aftermath of it all would be, heartbreak and devastation on Oak Ridge Plantation.

Just a few provisions would be enough. Sonders had insisted. Some bread, cheese, a chunk of pork bacon, maybe a bit of jam, and a few pats of butter and, of course, a canteen of hot steaming coffee. The intent was to make this look and feel like an aristocratic affair of them picnicking. Surely something Caroleena had enjoyed her fair share of in whatever previous life's experiences she actually did have before Sonders.

Sonders did not want the focus of their jaunt to be all about food anyway. This was just to set the stage. He had many things to say, and food would only get in his way, once he got started.

Lastly, he could not forget the most important piece to be added inside the hamper; the article of evidence that had come into his possession, just last night. Sonders tucked it in carefully, out of view, and he would not pull it out until the perfect moment presented itself.

*****

Caroleena was refreshed and ready to rise earlier than her normal day would have typically commenced before coming to Oak Ridge Plantation, but she did have a few things to do before going downstairs and seeing him.

She dressed with an extra layer for warmth, knowing she needed to be outside for part of this morning and with him alone. The climax of her scheme would come to life in a matter of hours now. And should everything go according to plan, the way she had watched it play out over and over in her mind, there was the strong likelihood that she may even get a wee bit wet; Black Mingo would see to that.

Caroleena would urge Sonders to take her on a carriage ride. Using her soft, kind voice and chosen sweet words would surely entreat him to want to go. Sonders could show her around the estate, possibly revisiting some of the same places and sights she had admired just yesterday. She could even pretend to be interested in his boyhood home and all of his shenanigans as a child, if that is what it would take. She could come across as looking fully involved in his life, in his world. Caroleena needed him to see that she was who he had fallen in love with, that poised, perfect, beautiful woman. No matter what it would take, she could fake it one last time.

Perfect as usual, she thought to herself. Caroleena paused at the balustrade, before descending the curved-oak staircase, hesitating long enough to gaze upon her own reflection in the tall, tortoiseshell-veneered mirror; imported from Italy, when the O'Rees first built the Big House. It had been strategically hung there many years ago for the house's residents to take that one last assessment of themselves, to make sure they were presentable for any situation that would be encountered on any given day. And, today, Caroleena Lumford Osgood O'Ree knew she was more than presentable; she was ready, able, and eager for what she had to accomplish, though she always thought this of herself. It had always been her way of life.

She had first noticed the object upon arriving at the Big House just three mornings earlier while being escorted to her lady's suite by Lucy. On a long highboy table off to the left of the wall mirror were a few sparkling vases arranged just so; one large urn displaying late winter, long-stemmed flowers, presumably from the garden here on

Oak Ridge Plantation, and more than likely kept filled by any floral growing season year-round. A brilliant painting of an expansive cotton field in full bloom with a gentleman's gentleman atop a spectacular horse, surely admiring his estate as he made rounds for that day, rested gently on a gold-plated easel, obviously displaying someone's apparent talent. A crystal decanter filled with some sort of light-brown whiskey and matching etched crystal glasses rested together awaiting the next partaker of a good and necessary drink; she was sure the decanter was filled with nothing but the best, of course.

Off to the back right edge of the highboy table, undoubtedly a showpiece, Caroleena had noticed a weighty glass globe that displayed a beautiful butterfly of reds and yellows and greens in its wings, encased somehow inside the glass; a feat that only a true artisan could have maneuvered, capturing the freed butterfly and trapping it behind a heavy wall of glass, all the while retaining the butterfly perfectly and beautiful and preserved.

Part of her well thought out and organized plans for this day involved slipping the heavy glass globe into her deep, inside cape pocket and going unnoticed, and it undetectable. The glass globe would do nicely for what she needed it for. Ogling it one more time gave her confirmation; this was the perfect object, an object for destruction.

Once snug, deep in the hidden inside pocket, Caroleena checked her gait to ensure her walk was not wobbled or unsteadied by the additional weight to her one side. Confident then, she approached and descended the staircase, finding Sonders standing there as if he had expected her at that exact moment in time.

Within seconds, and now standing side by side, Sonders gently placed his hand at the small of her back, causing Caroleena to recoil ever so slightly, catching her off guard but if only for a split second, hoping that he had not noticed. Sonders proceeded to tell her of a surprise he had arranged, a sort of "welcome to your new home" outing. They had not had much time alone since she had arrived at Oak Ridge Plantation, so this would be good for them, something they could do together, something that would be very special for them both; and this was his lure to get her in place for what he needed to accomplish.

Her mind raced wildly, thinking of her own plans and how this was going to affect every meticulous step she had put into place. Was she going to be able to carry out what needed to be done and done today? There was such a short window of time to conduct the plot or else she would have to go back to the proverbial drawing board and start all over.

Keeping control of her physical reaction, and thinking quickly on her feet, Caroleena kindly acknowledged his plans, accepting graciously the invitation to join him for some quality alone time; and adding that she, too, had something for him and had planned to give it to him today as well, and being alone was perfect for what she had hoped for. Little did either of them know, both their plans were similar yet with very different outcomes. In just a few more hours, everything would be changed on Oak Ridge Plantation, and changed for everyone.

Silas had slipped out the kitchen entrance, heading to the barn to ready both Boston and Diablo for their part in this morning's outing. With food hamper in tow, and the quilt to be used, Silas saddled and walked both beasts around to the front of the Big House. Thankfully, the rain had ceased with most of the fall already soaked into the sandy soil of this Low Country land.

Having taken her arm and wrapped it through his own, Sonders' had escorted Caroleena down the front porch stairs, gently and lovingly, trying not to expose his deep ire and dissatisfaction of this creature now latched on to him. The horses approached their mark, now whinnying from their excitement of a brisk morning ride. Sonders' stride put him ahead of Silas to assist Caroleena up and onto Diablo, while Silas held the saddle steady, leather reins in hand. And quick as a flash of lightning, Sonders was seated up high on Boston, waiting patiently for Silas to lay the quilt down first, then fastening the hamper to the saddle with a bit of roping. Stepping back, Silas popped both horses' hindquarters with a quick slap, and they were off for an adventure of a lifetime and for a story created by their escapade to be told for sure and for a long time to come.

*****

The shadow of a man had followed the two, doing his best to keep up considering he was on foot. Good thing Sonders had their horses in a slow walk, nothing more than a trot at times. His shadow was only visible to himself. No one else saw him. He had his reason. He knew his purpose.

CHAPTER 19

Grounds Work

Silas did his best to stay out of sight and out of the way of Sonders and Caroleena's course around the grounds. Sonders had explained his plan to a tee; Silas would simply be helping to execute it. Silas couldn't wait to get down to Black Mingo and scurry up into the arms of Uncle Henry, one of his favorite places on this entire plantation to be. He could see the world from here or so he could imagine.

Silas had been as far north as Charleston, down to Savannah and northwest to Spartanburg, but in Uncle Henry's arms, he could pretend to be anywhere in this great big world. There was no judgment about his sanity when he spoke of things to Uncle Henry; that maybe he was standing along the wharfs of the booming port of New York City, or pulling the rope to ring the Liberty Bell in Philadelphia, unbeknownst to him, just forty-five years later, it would receive its fatal crack that would keep it from ever ringing again.

But Silas loved imagining the moment when he set foot on his home land, Sierra Leone, South Africa; a place he had never seen but felt he knew it well from the many stories he had heard, passed down from his Mama Hattie and her Grandmamma Haney, who actually did come over to this new world on a slave ship, all the way from Sierra Leone. Fact was, most Sierra Leone slaves had been deported to the southeast coast of America, with almost 70 percent coming mainly to South Carolina. That's how Silas knew the whereabouts of his ancestors, where his maternal heritage was rooted. And that always seemed to bring a bit of comfort to him. Simply knowing made a difference. And today, his roots were anchored with the paternal bloodline of his brother, Sonders Josiah O'Ree.

Sometimes, as a child, when playing with Sonders, which was most of the time, Silas would pretend he was a pirate sailing on one of the biggest vessels in the world; and instead of robbing other boats, he would be the good guy and give his treasure away. This was a very important comparison of how Silas was so much like Sonders, linked by a moral heart, genuine to the core, so loving and kind.

Silas pondered on a few of these things before rescuing his mind back to the purpose of why he was up here today. It was not about anything else. There was just one reason and that was to be the eyes and the ears of what was going to happen here, and it would all be carried out very soon.

Today's mission was asking a lot of Silas and a lot more from Sonders. Together, these two would have to put aside everything good and decent and caring and try to see through the veil of tainted glasses, into the eyes of depravity and deceit.

Being so contrary to his nature, the only thought that helped Silas to focus was to continually keep reminding himself of all the wicked things that she had done, that she had brought here to Oak Ridge Plantation. And it seemed from the looks of that trunk and all that it contained, and with her killing that pitiful baby; well, thinking about what she was capable of helped him to concentrate all the more. This would all be over soon. Just had to be.

Now that Silas was positioned up high and out of sight, shielded by Uncle Henry's strong arms and the camouflage of dangling Spanish moss shrouding him, he sat back, nervous as a stray cat but ready to do his part.

*****

As morning birds continued their charming songs, the sun had been slowly making its presence into a now cloudless sky, drying up the heavy dew and burning off the low-lying fog that crept almost eerily along the sandy grounds just a few hours earlier, a much different view than what one would have imagined after a rainy night was now in view. The two horses trotted along easily; their riders admiring it all, appreciating the grandeur set out before them, giving them refuge from their racing minds of what was to come.

Passing by the early spring garden flower patch, Sonders reminded Caroleena of the beauties taken from here, and just for her, which had been arranged throughout the Big House on the day of her arrival to Oak Ridge Plantation. Sonders pointed out places where he had played as a young lad, almost always with Silas in tow and them trying to stay out of as much mischief as they knew to do as two young boys.

These were good experiences leaving Sonders with a warm feeling and very good memories. Nevertheless, ever present in his mind were the things Sonders had just learned about his beloved Caroleena that frightened him, angered him and, ultimately, had driven him to this point in time, what he must carry out, and it was just a matter of time now.

Just how much more about Caroleena did he not know scared Sonders, giving him a shiver of fright, of dread. How could he have been so naive and tricked by this wicked woman? Hopefully, he would find out before it was too late. He had to have some answers.

Caroleena was enjoying the ride with great anticipation building inside her gut, her mind, and obviously felt in her nerves as her entire body tingled with expectancy of finalizing her plan. With all her might, Caroleena allowed the cool fresh air to keep her internal temperatures down. She had to concentrate on every word Sonders was saying. She couldn't miss anything because everything would be of importance to her today for what she must do. And one day soon, she knew she would sell this magnificent plantation to its next owner. Caroleena knew all too well that she would be the one reaping the most benefit from the fallout of today.

The cool temperatures allowed for her to stay calm, to listen, to show Sonders that she was interested and, most importantly, to try to diffuse any suspicion that he may have developed for whatever reason about her and her purpose in his life. She was prepared mentally and physically. All too well, she knew that she would be able to do what she came here to do.

Riding down sandy lanes and rutted paths and out and across the lands of Oak Ridge Plantation would have brought a lot of pleasure to anyone so lucky to have such an experience, particularly with the one you loved. But this ride was different for both of them. Their minds were preoccupied with details and timing, completely different plans, but with similar thoughts traveling through each of their minds. While adrenaline flowed, moving them forward, faster than their horses could have ever run, Sonders and Caroleena were moved closer to the edge, to the end of good or evil. Which one would survive would soon be told.

His favorite spot along Black Mingo's banks was just in sight. At the same time, both excitement and fear gripped his heart tightly. The horses were brought to a stop. Caroleena's respirations were quick and breathy as she recognized this exact location from her escapade here just yesterday. Sonders had decided this was their stop, and she knew she was more than ready. This seemed now the perfect place for it all to commence, for it all to be finished.

Sonders dismounted Boston, tying the bridles of both Boston and Diablo to a low-lying limb of Uncle Henry, a loose-enough restraint for them to still wander to graze, but short enough to keep them nearby and ready. Gently and carefully, but with a disgust of hatred for this woman, Sonders assisted Caroleena off Diablo, handing her the quilt to hold while he unbound the breakfast hamper from Boston. Walking just a few steps away from Uncle Henry and closer to Black Mingo's water's edge, Sonders exclaimed this was the perfect spot, just as planned. Caroleena thought to herself, *Oh, my dear, you just don't know how perfect.*

Caroleena, believing that Sonders was still smitten by her, sashayed over to the spot where Sonders had spread out the quilt, walking with an exaggerated flounce to her step, hoping to catch his eye of passion. Sitting down ever so gracefully but yet cautiously as to not give away what was hidden in her cape pocket, she motioned for Sonders to join her.

The rushing sound of Black Mingo's waters was all that could be heard, and every so often, a fine cool mist wafted in the air to find rest on their faces and hands. Black Mingo took over these next few moments in time, taking center stage in their minds, diverting them for a brief respite from the reality of why they were actually here. The beauty of this place, oh how distracting it was. As the two watched and listened intently, eyes gazing and ears pealed, the small splashes of white-capped waves that Black Mingo provided were likened to a theatrical play, luring them both to a place not here but somewhere off in a distant land. Black Mingo was mesmerizing as if they were both put into a trance, under a spell from Black Mingo's power. The waters had that sort of control as if it were alive and had a soul of its own and with a purpose.

Nibbling on the prepared breakfast, sipping the piping hot coffee, and sitting quietly, these first few moments together passed by slowly, almost too slowly. Sonders wanted all the facts laid out on the table. He was ready. He was deserving. Caroleena wanted the tables to be turned for her own plans to commence and, with perfect timing, they would.

Sonders began talking about all that they had seen along their outing: the lane going back toward the road that led into the Village where rows of live oak trees lined the landscape, his great-grandfather, Allister, had played here as a boy, and these trees were old even then. Sonders had heard stories of how the trees were masterfully and purposefully planted so as to grow into this large canopy of limbs and interlocking arms above the lane to be a purposed and meaningful welcoming entrance to anyone who might venture onto this property of Oak Ridge Plantation.

Sonders exclaimed how he hoped it had welcomed her, too, all the while still attempting to give Caroleena the illusion that all was well when, in reality, nothing was right with this world. Sonders now had his own masterfully and purposefully planned-out scheme, and she would very soon be finding out all about it.

CHAPTER 20

The Confrontation

With tides now turned, Sonders moved the conversation to the paths Caroleena had not discovered on her own just the day before. Sonders pointed out the big barn, where cotton was kept after being picked in the fields. He pointed out that by blood and sweat from so many is what it had taken to fill this barn each and every year, with this last year being the best seen in Oak Ridge Plantation's record keeping yet.

His next planned-out, one-sided conversation was to remind her of their halt at the Woodshed, where Sonders had purposely stopped, pointedly noting to Caroleena some of the horrors that had occurred there, even death, when he was not yet the Planter of Oak Ridge Plantation. Sonders' intent was to raise the hair a bit on the back of the nape of Caroleena's neck, wanting her to be uncomfortable, hoping she was prickled by his alluding to a similar outcome for her if so deserving. Sonders believed he had succeeded. He had observed Caroleena readjusting her body on the quilt, not from sitting there too long but from an irritated sting that he had wielded, and he had hit the bull's-eye.

As they both listened to the loud, rushing waters of Black Mingo, Sonders recognized its levels were actually high now, not just from the overnight's rainfall but also because of high tide that the Atlantic Ocean was currently at, controlling Black Mingo with its ebbs and flows. Black Mingo's waters appeared to be breeching its bank, but Sonders knew better; Caroleena would not. Sonders knew what the undertow and faster current in the river would feel like once in. It could be a scary experience if not prepared for it. Sonders could only hope this to be the case for Caroleena.

*****

With the object she had so carefully handpicked from inside the Big House and had secluded in her cape, Caroleena felt it turn ever so slightly as she repositioned herself, not from being rattled from his obvious insinuation of fear but from needing to be readied, to stand from this sitting position, once the time was right. The glass globe would be heavy enough, she mused, rounded enough and properly blunt enough to work its purpose, just when she was going to need it most.

With breakfast nibbling over, the time now was going by quickly, and her excitement and anticipation of what lay ahead was now in sight, giving her that extra surge of energy she would need to see herself through what she would have to do to bring about this next step in her plan. She was in the clear. Full steam ahead.

*****

With light conversation turning quickly into much deeper exchange, the clock was ticking for both of them. Both knew it was time to begin.

Sonders told Caroleena that he wanted to know so much more about her, that their love was so young, and that there was so much more to learn, and what better time to start learning than right here and right now. Caroleena leaned in and replied that she, too, wanted to know more about him, but that he should go first. She knew what she wanted to say and exactly how she was going to start.

Sonders tone changed slightly, with a bit of quivering in his lower lip, and detected in his voice but only if you knew him well enough. He proceeded to ask Caroleena about Majestic Oaks Plantation and her time growing up there as a child.

A bit agitated, Caroleena reminded him that she had previously told him about her childhood and time growing up there, that Mother and Father had been the crux of society, that she literally had nothing to worry over, that she had had a good life. Mother had succumbed to the delivery of twins; and Father was left to run Majestic Oaks Plantation alone, after she went off to higher learning in Philadelphia. Caroleena continued with a few more details confirming what Sonders had heard before until he stopped her.

Needing this escapade to accelerate, Sonders fast-forwarded through their prior conversation that they had in Charleston by recalling some of the events for her. He listed her schooling, her returning from Philadelphia married, and that within days of being at Majestic Oaks Planation, both her father and husband, Desmond, had succumbed to that horrible accident on the staircase. Angrily Sonders recounted, the estate had caught fire later, burning completely to the ground. Her twin sisters had succumbed to their deaths in that estate fire. Understandably, Sonders was now very skeptical of Caroleena and her Charlestonian story.

Through weeping and sobbing and an abundance of shed tears, Caroleena had explained then that she could not stand the thought of remaining in Spartanburg, and from having lost so much, so given the opportunity by Delia, her good friend, she left for Charleston and to a new life there.

Sonders pointed out that he had been disappointed the night of her arrival to Oak Ridge Plantation, when she had excused herself early for the night, leaving him alone, the banquet planned just for her, and all their guests a bit confused, wondering what could have been awry. He added, though, he was glad she went to refresh herself for the special time that they did spend together later that night, alone.

For the first time, Sonders spoke of the couple who had arrived late that night to the banquet, Mr. and Mrs. Harlan and Josephine Humphries, who were sorely disappointed to not meet his new bride, the fair and lovely Caroleena. The Humphries were the new planters of Majestic Oaks Plantation. Sonders paused here long enough and then said, "Purchased from a Caroleena Lumford Osgood." As he spoke this, Sonders watched carefully for any sign of discomfort as he knew now that the estate had not burned. It didn't take much concentration as he noted a catch in Caroleena's breath, a slight flush to her face, a quick dart of her eyes as if she were trying to think about how to counter what she had just heard.

Though Caroleena had told Sonders that Majestic Oaks Plantation had burned to the ground, the Humphries gleefully told Sonders and all the guests gathered that night about how beautiful the long-existing estate was, and that they were so pleased to be the new planters of Majestic Oaks Plantation. And yet it was Yosef Eckstein who just yesterday mentioned that the sale of this grand upstate plantation was to a Caroleena Lumford Osgood.

Without giving her one split second to recoil to his first disclosure, Sonders moved quickly into his next discovery of that same night where Caroleena had been too close to an unladylike advancement toward a strange gentleman on the portico, when she had needed to step out for a bit of fresh air, at least that was how she had explained it to him then.

Uneasiness was written all over Caroleena, but she quickly dismissed that notion retorting and scolding him for even thinking such a thing, that she only had eyes for him. Snapping back, Sonders told Caroleena quickly that Silas had been outside and had seen her moving seductively forward, toward a gentleman, one of the guests from the evening's banquet. He had seen this man moving toward Caroleena, in anticipation of an embrace, a sexually charged expression had graced his face.

Squirming, Caroleena quickly denied such, stating that Silas was just a slave and that he had totally misunderstood anything that he may or may not have seen on that portico. How anyone could believe a slave over her was commencing from her lips, of course, speaking defense for herself, but Sonders had other things needing to be said, and he immediately stopped her. He knew the next two accounts could not be so easily denied or contradicted by the woman holding his heart. All the love he once had for her was quickly being sucked out and replaced with hatred and disgust.

Sonders had moved around, squatting now on one knee, the other leg up and ready to stand in an instant. This was something Caroleena could not deny. He searched for the correct words and blurted them out, asking about the locked trunk that Lucy and Silas had discovered in her closet. And the key hidden inside her pillowcase. Sonders knew the sort of items in the trunk but kept that close to his chest, at least for now. Caroleena snapped back that it was just full of old things from her childhood, from the academy, memorabilia that she had held on to and had kept it locked for safe travels as she came from Spartanburg to Charleston and now here to Graham Village and to Oak Ridge Plantation.

Lies upon lies, and with each exposure of what he had learned being brought into the light and being refuted by her at every turn, Sonders stood, fully upright now, livid and fuming with anger, he called her hand at all this with raised voice. "Then what is the answer to all of the contents inside that trunk Caroleena? The gems? The money? The gold? Not at all like you have just described, Caroleena!"

Rising from her seated position, Caroleena was now red flushed and raging with formed fists. She was visibly shaken, trembling but silent. There wasn't anything she could say about what Sonders had just confronted her with. She had nothing to say, which was exactly how Sonders thought she would react.

Both now standing, Sonders proceeded with the final blow of facts, knowing before he spoke that this would be the clincher. Ever so slowly, Sonders had been advancing them both toward the river's edge, Caroleena in total oblivion to understand what he was doing or to how dangerously close she was positioned now to the rushing waters. All she could hear in her mind was that this was not how she had planned today's play, this was not at all what she wanted to happen, and she didn't know how to make it stop.

Eyes now blazing red, fury written all over his countenance and so angry that hot tears welled up in his eyes, Sonders growled, "How could you? Who are you?"

Still within arm's reach of the breakfast hamper, Sonders bent down, lifted its lid, and yanked out the bloodied apron that he and Silas found in this exact spot only yesterday. Shaking it wildly and within inches of her face, he screamed, "He was a newborn! A tiny defenseless human being just born, umbilical cord still attached. What did you do?"

Sonders looked completely out of control, though he knew exactly what he was doing. Caroleena could feel Sonders' hot steaming breath. He was that close now. Still holding the bloodied apron, Sonders' strong hands gripped her shoulders, and he began shaking her violently, screaming that this was not all the proof of what she had done. He expected she would try to talk herself out of this charge as well, just as she had with every other accusation he had approached her with.

Caroleena was shell-shocked, stunned, distraught as to how this was playing out. Caroleena had absolutely no control over anything. Sonders had proof of all that she had lied about, covered up all these years, of everything. And for the first time in her life, Caroleena was speechless, clueless as to how to proceed. Dumbfounded, she opened her mouth, but no words would come.

Ever so slightly, the two had been advancing into Black Mingo's cold water. Now ankle deep, they stood, pushing against his will, Caroleena attempted to loosen his grip, but he held all the more tightly. Sonders last blow was that he had found the infant. The body was still in Black Mingo's waters, trapped, pitiful soul, drowned, and for no reason. He and Silas had helped Amos bury the baby, along with his mother last night, in the gloom of a lost night, dark and lonely.

This was the first time Caroleena had heard that the baby's mother had died. That had not been her intent at all. Caroleena knew that her usual feelings about such would have been a calm reaction internally but now knew to exude a surprised reaction for him to see as an appropriate reaction from a lady. This time, there was no use to pretend. Though being caught off guard and being more than rattled, Caroleena grappled for words. Her words. Her true-self words.

What reason could she possibly have had? None. Absolutely none. There was nothing in this world that should bring one human being to take an infant from its mother and to drown it! There was absolutely nothing that she could say, and nothing she would say that would make him understand. She had been caught. Now there was only one thing she could do; Caroleena would have to tell Sonders the truth, the entire mess of the truth.

A tiny squeak fell from her mouth; Sonders lowered his head closer to hers, bending his ear to attempt to understand what she was trying to say. But there was nothing to say. With all his might, his greater strength pushed her backward, falling further away from shore and into deeper, colder rushing water. Going under and quickly coming back up, Caroleena gasped, choked, and sputtered that she was only a slave. And that baby was just a perpetuation of a slave. It didn't matter was what she had to say.

Coughing out water that had found its way into her nose and mouth and wiping her eyes from the brown opaque water dripping ferociously from all over her head, Caroleena had come up from the waters with a new expression he had not seen before; her facial features had become demon-like; her countenance was exuding all the evil that had lurked inside her for much too long.

Fueled now by the raging adrenaline flowing throughout his body, and the realization from the exposure of truth had obviously meant nothing to her. Every truth he had exposed was only to be denounced by more lies. Sonders pushed his way out into deeper water, using his free arm like the oar of a boat, further out with Caroleena. Grabbing both of her arms and shaking her violently, Sonders pleaded for her response. Before this could end, Sonders had to know why!

Yelling through his own madness, he shouted that she was a liar, the spawn of evil, that she could never make up enough lies to get her through this masquerade that she had been living and tricking everyone in her path and, more than likely, for her entire life. There would be absolutely nothing she could say, no reason to defend all that she had done, and what he knew she had done surely only scratched the surface of what someone like her could have done in a lifetime. Sonders could not imagine what was in her wake, her past. There must be something hauntingly deplorable, an absolutely horrifying event that made her into this beast.

Black Mingo was now playing its part in their schemes. As if on cue, Black Mingo's current assisted Sonders by sweeping them both out into her deeper, more challenging waters. Caroleena was quickly losing the battle. Neither could find good footing. Black Mingo's icy cold water was taking its toll on them both. Even Sonders was finding it difficult to stay upright. Black Mingo had her own plans, and neither Sonders nor Caroleena could fight against it.

Going under himself a couple of times before finding his steadiness, Sonders was reminded of his mission, his purpose, the only logical reason he could remind himself of for being out in Black Mingo like this and at this time of year. Against his will and who he was at his core, Sonders was reminded of the task at hand, to make this all go away, to end, and it would be by his hands. Caroleena would not be coming out of Black Mingo's hold alive.

Caroleena had lost all control at this point. Her entire effort was put into staying alive. She had to fight with everything in her, with everything she had. Her will and her purpose was to come out of this so that she could carry out her own plans, those of taking him down. And with one last surge of strength, Caroleena pushed herself up and out of Black Mingo's death grip, her watery hold. Choking and gasping for a breath, Caroleena screamed the word, "Enough!"

CHAPTER 21

Irrelevant Admissions

As Sonders held Caroleena down, under Black Mingo's cold, dark waters, he could feel the fight still remaining in this creature. Her strength amazed him, actually caught him off guard by her power. Not much ever surprised Sonders, but this woman had done nothing but that since the moment he first laid eyes on her.

Caroleena continued to battle. She had to break through his hold. She had to survive. She had accomplished too much in her twenty-five years of life, proven herself to so many, mainly to herself that she wasn't about to let all of this go down without her best fight ever.

With the strength and tenacity of a den of lions, she resolved that she would live. Caroleena surged forward against Sonders's hold, and with one last push, she mustered up one final thrust, bringing herself up to the top of the rushing, raging waters, waves swelling all around her mightily, intensely, but evidently not as strong as she had just proven herself to be.

A despicable river monster erupted through the churning waves of Black Mingo. Surging up from under the river's driving, muddy waters and out on top of her rapids of white-capped breakers, Caroleena's talons raked across and into his neck, his face, his arms, digging in, bringing forth a slow stream of O'Ree blood, deep crimson-red flowing now from his body, his wounds. She struggled to use him as her anchor, to pull herself up and out of the water, trying to latch onto anything, gasping and grasping for any semblance of life. He was fighting her every move. More importantly, his life hinged on the struggle, hung in the balance of who the victor would be in this fight.

Enough was her first word she was able to sputter out! Sonders retained his tight hold but loosened his grip enough that she understood she was being given a chance, a chance to live, a chance to speak at least for now. Sonders must have thought this or else he would not have hesitated for her to continue. He could have pushed her further down into the depths of Black Mingo and completed the path he was already on.

Caroleena was convinced, believed that Sonders knew enough, and what he knew would destroy her, along with everything that she had planned for up until now. She still had a chance. She had to scramble to tell him in time or else he was going to kill her, and she still had plans of her own in the works.

It was time, time to finally tell all. No one in this entire world knew it all, but she recognized Sonders now would. And the best place to start was at the beginning, and with truth to be told.

*****

Her waters strengthened and rushed stronger than just an hour earlier. The currents were churning, and Black Mingo seemed somehow disappointed in the change of tides, annoyed, angered, was in some way possibly saddened by the change in heart of Sonders and Caroleena, that she wasn't going to collect on another life today. But there was always hope. This is what the mighty river had grown accustomed to, taking life and swallowing it up, hopefully nevermore to be remembered. But the day was still young. Black Mingo had hoped to add another story to her waters where hiding secrets living behind her walls of water was life to her, sustenance to keep flowing. If only others knew that there were ghostlike figures now existing in her waters, they would be horrified. Ghosts and death were her secrets to keep.

*****

Doing their best to stand in Black Mingo's enraged waters, Caroleena found herself holding to Sonders' forearm tightly with both hands, just to be sure that she wouldn't be let go by him and swept away by the river. She urged Sonders to please take them both into shallower waters where they would have more stability. She begged for this, assuring him that she would tell him everything. She found herself pleading, and words such as these never came out of Caroleena Lumford Osgood O'Ree's mouth. She was scared; defeat was looming on the horizon, and she saw it full-on coming for her.

Wading a bit closer to shore, sure footing being found by them both, Sonders refused to go any closer to Black

Mingo's shoreline. He insisted that she start talking, and she had better explain herself and now.

Caroleena began. She had led a sheltered life, was given anything she could ever want or hope or ask for. The wealth of the Lumfords had made sure of that. She was an only child and born with a strong and stubborn will. She admittedly took advantage of that. She could pout and get her way. She learned she could scream, rant, or rage, showing tantrums, and Mother or Father would yield to her fancy every single time. No slave would deprive her of whatever she wanted nor stop her from what she could and would do. The world was her kite, and she held the string; everything and everyone was wrapped around her finger.

She was twelve years old when it had happened. It was the worst nightmare anyone could ever fathom, and she had it happen to her. Caroleena sometimes would pretend it was just that, a very bad dream. She would try to escape the horror, but that never worked. She physically had tried to escape him, but that, too, was not possible. Mother and Father never knew; in fact, no one knew until now. Sonders would be the first and the only one to ever know what had happened to the young lady Caroleena, except for him. '"I was raped!"

Caroleena stopped speaking but, for a moment, reflecting on that day, the day she was raped. Father never came to her rescue. Though he didn't know, she still blamed Father for not being there for her. He had not been there when she needed him the most. Father had to pay, and so he did. The fall on the staircase was no accident, and Desmond had gone down with him too. Just like all the men she encountered in her schemes, they all had to pay.

Wild-eyed and continuing on, Caroleena spoke, attempting to play on all the good that she knew was in him. She pathetically told Sonders that when she thought life was leaving her body, just moments before, when Sonders had her held beneath Black Mingo's waters, she felt for the first time ever an escape, a relief, or release, that she was finally fleeing the hands of that horrible nightmare.

Screaming and crying so loud that even the sounds of Black Mingo's waters seemed muffled by her cries, Caroleena opened up for the first time since it had happened. She had been raped. She yelled, brutally and violently raped. The reality in her life was that she had been sadistically brutalized.

Sonders's grip released ever so slightly. Somehow compassion was finding a wee place in his heart, once filled with such a strong love for her now soured and turned to hate; he needed to hear more. Realizing that she could go on, Caroleena continued, sobbing and crying and reliving every second of those moments at the hands of that man. She spoke loudly and coarsely. And then almost whispered, uttering softly and pathetically as the remembrance of the horrid act drained her.

After what seemed like hours, Caroleena finally was able to yell out that had Father only known it was one of his work hands, someone earning his living at the expense of her father's purse. He had taken advantage of not only her but also of Father. He would have dealt with him, and it would not have gone very well for that man. And that man was Frederick Barber!

This was not fair. And Caroleena had determined that his crime would not go unpunished. What this man did was distorted and perverted and sick and maddening, and the experience had changed her forever. It made her into who she had become. Sonders was believing Caroleena for the first time. He saw truth in her eyes and on her face. She wasn't lying anymore. He was sure of that.

Caroleena went on that she had decided then and there that no man would ever do this to her again, ever! No man would ever have control over her ever again. And that she would never be in the shadows of a man, in any form or fashion, societally, financially, educationally, or in any thing or in any way. She would have power; she would be sure to have wealth and status and position, and everything any man had, she would take. Just like this man had taken from her the most valuable thing that she had, she would make sure to take from all men everything that they had. Even if it meant taking lives down, she didn't care. No man would ever again harm her.

Sonders was standing in the river, listening intently, shaking all over, and right down to his boots. This was all too surreal. He urged her to continue. Sonders needed to know it all, no matter the cost.

Caroleena cried that if it meant seeking out the love of any man whose path crossed with hers, and she deemed him fit for her plans of advancement, then so be it. It didn't matter the pain, the heartache, or the loss of a life. Sonders knew that she was referring to him now. Caroleena was going to win, and win every time she did. And Sonders was to be no exception.

Caroleena finally spoke the words to seal her fate. She said it again, that Sonders would be no exception. She had admitted that she had seen him on New Year's Eve, and though he was an attractive man, she saw him to be the perfect fit as the next cog in her wheel of advancement to her plan. Ultimately having it all: wealth, power, position, fortune, and fame. She had left the twin brats completely destitute after the sale of Majestic Oaks Plantation, and now Oak Ridge Plantation was next on her list.

Getting Sonders to fall in love with her had been easy, almost too easy. And here they were, just weeks into the new year and already at the point of her gaining the fortune and position of owning Oak Ridge Planation; why it had almost caught her by surprise as to just how easy. It had happened all so fast. It had been perfect. She admitted it had been fun, fascinating to have all the doting and adoration Sonders unleashed on her, sparing no expense. With every move he made, every dollar spent, Caroleena received affirmation that Sonders was the one.

She had left too many things in her past obviously with a crack left open in the door. She thought she had closed all the loopholes. But unbeknownst to her, people had talked, events had occurred, or so she was explaining. She had escaped from the horrors and from the memories of Majestic Oaks Plantation, but its ghosts had followed her right here and into these wildly rushing waters of Black Mingo.

And so there they were. Waist-deep in water and shoulders deep in decisions to be made. Sonders had heard enough. It was all very clear that he had only been used. Caroleena was as dastardly as anyone he had ever known. Immoral. Corrupt and evil and wicked to the core, and this had to end.

Pushing out again into the deep, Sonders had Caroleena by the shoulders, and she knew it was too late to stop him. She pleaded with him that she had told him the truth, but it was the truth that tripped the switch for Sonders to continue on with the knowledge that evil had to die. He could not and would not let this go on.

And, once again, out in Black Mingo's rushing, deeper waters, Sonders plunged the beautiful and fair Caroleena down and under, against the raging current, feeling the fight leave her body, listening as the gurgling in her throat diminished behind the sounds of Black Mingo's swishing and whirling waves, watching for the last bubbles to trickle up to the surface of Black Mingo's waters, indicating that life had been extinguished; there was no more. Caroleena was departed now from this world. Evil had finally been snuffed out and, at last, Oak Ridge Plantation was given her salvation once again.

CHAPTER 22

Murky Waters

Black Mingo was listening to the last sounds of Caroleena's gurgles creeping out of her lungs and stealing up her throat, proving that the end was only seconds away. Her splashes and thrashing were weakening, waning, just distant gulps and sucks with no pattern to their timing was all that was left, was all Caroleena had left in her. The hungry waters hoped it would be soon a quick death.

The river's insatiable appetite for human life was running on empty, and Caroleena Lumford Osgood O'Ree would refuel Black Mingo for a long time to come. Sin and darkness such as hers was a godsend, providing a fueling, a satisfaction that this river had not known in a very long time.

But something wasn't quite right. Black Mingo was still wrestling with this life. Caroleena's ghost was suspended somewhere between existence and the hereafter. Black Mingo would just need to be patient. She would eventually succumb. She just had to wait. All the river had was time.

*****

As Sonders held Caroleena's body under the murky waters, he looked into her frantic eyes, leering at her, through the struggles of holding her down, weighting her body down with his own mass. It became less and less of a struggle as the seconds passed.

Sonders thought aloud, "Love is strange, love is hard, this hurts so much." Sonders ached from head to toe, and his heart was breaking completely in two. He had to let her go.

Such a down sliding in such a short amount of time was mind-boggling. Sonders had only known Caroleena for a little over a month, but had he known her at all? His "to have and to hold until death parts them" had become unnatural and violent. Sonders had wanted to be her everything, and now he had been. He had rescued her, rescued her from herself, from harming anyone else, especially him. In light of his plan, Sonders had wanted nothing more than restoration to who he once thought her to be, but that was evidently an impossible plea to ask of God. She was beyond saving.

Sonders was holding on now to only her hand and trying ever so hard to let go of her heart. He knew it was time to release Caroleena, to let Black Mingo take over, to do with her as her waters calculated. Sonders was making what he must do easier by finally letting go.

Turning toward the shoreline, striding the best he could against the strong current, swimming with his arms, rowing himself toward some stable foothold, Sonders was audibly talking to himself about who had he become. This was all Sonders could muster in his mind now. Letting go of his once-beloved Caroleena was not so easy a task. But he had to say goodbye. Treading away from her and moving back to Black Mingo's banks, he muttered aloud that it was over, evil vanished once again from Oak Ridge Plantation.

The loudness of the waters gave him camouflage. His conscience screaming concealed him from all reality, and talking aloud to himself was only a distraction. Sonders was in another world, a different place, possibly a place where he may not so easily return from. He was broken in every possible form or fashion that one person could ever be.

*****

Suddenly and wildly, thrashing and gasping, choking and coughing, this pale, white-washed creature arose up and out, onto the top of the rushing wild waters of Black Mingo, like the dead being resurrected, Caroleena was alive. Demon-like, red-streaked eyes now prominent from tiny broken blood vessels apparent from the torture they had just experienced, and a maddened fury of a being technically consumed and defeated by the waters, gave her acuity to continue with her plan in a new way, but still with the objective she had intended, to end Sonders Josiah O'Ree.

Eerily and strangely like a Cheshire cat with nine lives, Caroleena struggled to stay atop, but she knew she had won; above the waters was much easier to maneuver than from where she had just escaped his clutches and the river's control. With new focus, she saw her target just ahead, Sonders.

Fingers frantically struggling to find the glass globe, it was there, still secured deep within her cape pocket. Caroleena grabbed the object, securing it in her now-clasped hand, fingers holding tightly, never to let go. Assured that it was nested securely in hand, Caroleena advanced forward. She had risen up and out of Black Mingo's hold; one battle won, now feeding her, fueling her forward with a new rush of adrenaline, fire seethed within her and pure hatred and rage for this man pushed her onward; the final battle would also be won.

Sonders was completely oblivious that she was still alive, much less now moving rapidly through the waters and toward him. His mind, his thoughts, his everything were consumed. Nothing could have interrupted his solitary march back to shore. Absolutely nothing.

As if given a new lease on life, Caroleena knew she had to complete what she had started, what she had come here to do. It was her turn now. Her plans would be on display. Her distorted objectives would be fulfilled. She would win. He would lose. Period.

Breath now feeding air into her lungs, adrenaline nourishing her biological needs, and her evil mind convincing her to press on, with every step, Caroleena was shortening the distance between them. She was moving closer and closer to him, her target, the target. This would all soon be over. Caroleena was now more motivated with hatred and resentment than she had ever felt for anyone. Her plan had almost been squashed, nearly ruined by this man. He would not get away with it. Sonders would pay.

The edges of Black Mingo still lapping at his feet, Sonders had found refuge from the waters. Standing.

Shaking violently. Completely ruined by the act that he had just committed. Murder. Sin. Sonders Josiah O'Ree had actually murdered someone, had taken life that was only God's to take. Sonders was beside himself. All he could do was to cry. He cried out to his Lord. He cried with all the might that remained in him.

Within an arm's length from him now, Caroleena found her sure footing in the more shallow edge of Black Mingo's waters. Approaching, now quiet as a church mouse so as to not alarm or notify him of her presence, she needed to catch him off guard. Taking the glass globe in her right hand, and raising her arm high…

*****

Seeing her reappear from what he thought was a drowned body and advancing ever so quickly toward Sonders, Silas scurried down the tree as fast as he could. Trying not to bring harm to himself, he knew his brother would need him whole and well. Silas couldn't just leap down or else possibly sustain a broken bone and be useless to Sonders when he would need him the most.

Not knowing clearly now what he was seeing as he extracted himself from the hanging moss and Uncle Henry's limbs, the distance away from Black Mingo prevented Silas' screams from being heard, or so he thought. Caroleena had heard them and was only moved to advance all the more quickly to complete this deed, to bring this all to an end.

With all her might and strength, Caroleena slammed the raised object hard and fast into the back of Sonders' head, screaming and growling and listening for the sound of bone crunching, all of which brought her great pleasure into her wicked soul. Silas had been desperately attempting to distract this wild beast from her prey but to no avail.

The glass globe hit its mark. Staggering and screeching and wobbling now, with no control, the blow ultimately knocked Sonders down. His body sprawled out onto the ground, Sonders appeared to be knocked out, semiconscious.

Caroleena did not know who had been screaming, but she had a good idea; that brother of his, Silas. Her coward husband must have known he couldn't do this to her alone, would need someone to help him succeed at killing her or trying to, that is. Having Silas nearby had obviously been a part of his plan to do away with her. Well, Silas would be sorry too. Before turning her attention to this unwanted intruder into their personal affairs, Caroleena knew one last blow was necessary to end Sonders Josiah O'Ree and to make all of this officially hers.

Raising her arm one last time, the heavy glass globe still in hand, a few red markings of Sonders' blood streaked across and around the object now, Caroleena was ready to wield the final blow. Lowering herself ever so slightly to reach his body that now lay on the ground, Caroleena was coming down hard and fast with the intent to unleash the lethal impact. His hand caught her wrist, abruptly stopping it in midair, stilled and kept from striking the additional and final blow.

Silas had grabbed her wrist hard and purposefully. Tightly, wrenching it firmly and hoping to wield his own harm to her; he didn't care. He wrestled her to the ground, weighting her down by laying on top of her torso, arms, and legs. There they both lay, next to Sonders' body. Silas called out to his brother, fear in his voice, scared that it may be too late.

What seemed like forever, Sonders finally moved his legs, his arms, fingers digging into the damp, sandy soil. He pulled himself forward and up. Guttural sounds like a badly wounded dog erupted from Sonders as he grunted and moaned. Reaching for the back of his head, Sonders' fingers searched for the open wound, now flowing deep-red blood from the blow.

Dazed and floundering around, Sonders was now on his feet but stumbling. The blow had obviously worked as she intended, at least partly. His head was exploding. His sight was blurred, and his stability all affected by the strike. Trying to steady himself, Sonders was filled with fury and ire as he caught glimpse of Silas lying on the ground, right beside the spot where he had just risen from. Sonders couldn't logically make sense of this. He could not understand what had happened.

And it was then that he saw her underneath Silas, moving and thrashing about. To his shock and surprise, there was Caroleena—obviously alive, writhing like a snake to escape but with nowhere to go.

Her screams and pleadings for help could now have been heard all over the estate, if not for the sounds of Black Mingo muffling them to almost silent cries. Sonders heard them. Silas did too. And together they knew this had to be finished and, this time, completely finished. And by the two of them working together.

There were not enough words to describe how Sonders felt knowing that she had survived. He thought her dead for sure, when he had seen the last bubbles of life, had felt the last resistance of her fight in his arms. He was certain that he had left her in the murky, cold waters of Black Mingo, dead.

Sonders bent to take hold of Caroleena, allowing Silas to roll off her and get himself up. He yanked her up by the hands, her full weight being jerked up by his brutal force. Sonders wrapped his arms around her body, securing her tightly until Silas could position himself to stand in front of her. This time, the life would be choked out of her with the force of two grown men, and her cries would get lost in the swells and sounds of Black Mingo. Brothers would work together to ensure that Black Mingo took her this time. Black Mingo would fill her lungs, would suffocate Caroleena to death in her waters; she would go to a watery grave and disappear in Black Mingo's currents. They would let the river do the rest. Caroleena would finally be lost forever and dead.

As the three turned to face Black Mingo, they slowly approached the splashing edge of her waters. Black Mingo's waters almost looking impatient, wave after wave lapping at their feet as if she was welcoming them back into her waters. Resisting with all her might, Caroleena turned her body against the strength of both Silas and Sonders, almost escaping their tight grips when, out of nowhere... *Boom!*

As slow as a moving freight train approaching the station in Yemassee at the end of its long journey, the shot had been made; the bullet had escaped its chamber. Unleashed, the projectile was coming at them. The blast roaring in their ears, ringing vibrations throughout their heads. It was as if the shot had been fired right beside their heads and all control was lost. The bullet traveled. Saying the word slow motion was too fast for the approach of the bullet. Wild-eyed, there was no time to react. There was no place to go. And with all three souls lunging their best to avoid the bullet, it found its mark. With a direct hit, dead center of the forehead, the bullet penetrated its prey; knocking all three of them backward and off their feet and into the water's edge.

Caroleena was dead. Surely this time dead. The bullet had seen to that. She now lay in the water's edge from the fatal wound. Blood oozed from the hole now in her head. Brain matter seeping up and out of her skull, now laying on her brow. Black Mingo's waters lapped at the blood with each wave that ebbed and flowed, slurping up the now congealing blood, like a thirsty dog licking at the essence from a carcass of a forest animal not long ago deceased. Eyes wide open, blond hair wispily floating around her once beautiful face, Caroleena was staring at Sonders as if she had one final plea that would now never be spoken.

The brothers jumped up, searching for where the shot had come from. Who could have done this? Who knew that they were down here at the river, trying to rid this place of evil?

And as they were searching frantically for the answer, he emerged from behind Uncle Henry's thickest low-lying limb. He had hidden himself out of sight, behind the tree, had seen this entire scene play out from beginning to end, the end brought about by him, with his gun and his intent.

Sonders had not taken life from his beloved Caroleena. He had been spared that. He was saved from committing that sin. And there was some relief to his mind that he quickly found, but who had killed her? And why?

As the shadow of the man approached the gruesome scene, Sonders and Silas stood beside the lifeless body of the once fair and beautiful Caroleena. Anxiously waiting and readying themselves for a possible hit to either of them, the brothers recognized him. They had seen this man before, many times. This was evil. He was evil. This man was Frederick Barber. Evil had now rooted itself again deeper into the sandy soil here on Oak Ridge Plantation.

Evil died that day, but a different kind of wickedness had come home to roost.

EPILOGUE

Uncle Henry wept. He had seen too much. Destruction. Deceit. Death. From his place here, along the banks of Black Mingo, the tree had experienced it all, and for much too long now. Devastation had flowed past him, streaming over his deep and massive roots of anchor and of refuge. All that history now overlooking the murky waters of Black Mingo was logged into the book of antiquity, and nothing could change any of it.

Uncle Henry's tears trickled off his long limbs and branches, large droplets forming and dripping down into Black Mingo's waters. Her mouth was wide open, feeding her with more sorrow and grief than she certainly did not need or deserve but would lap up to relish. The turmoil that had bathed his roots over the history of time was overwhelming to the tree's soul.

Uncle Henry had been here for as long as he could remember. He recalled Sonders' father, Mordecai, and his brother, Barnabas, playing in his limbs, scurrying up and down and out and about, which had brought so much pleasure to the tree.

And likewise, his father, Haymoth, and the boyhood shenanigans played out in the shadows of Uncle Henry's trunk; such grand times the tree now reflected upon. It was his father, Allister, who built the Big House in 1691. Those were special days for sure.

Oh, all the joys that the tree had experienced through its time here in the Low Country of South Carolina. Uncle Henry reflected upon all the memories now logged in his mind. The tree was certainly glad for all the delights but, here of late, the pain and sorrows seemed to engulf him beyond the memories of happiness.

Uncle Henry was here when Oak Ridge Planation was erected, full-on into maturity even then, probably close to seventy-five years old or thereabouts. The tree recollected that as a special time when Allister and his brothers rested under Uncle Henry's trunk of limbs, a respite from the hot sun of summer days, and a break from cold winter winds that sometimes were a bit unbearable, even here in the Low Country of the South, all the while the Big House was being built, and oh, what a special and delightful time that had been for all.

But fast-forwarding to now, the tree reflected on more recent wretched times, the drowning of Barnabas and Emma, that poor little newborn baby murdered, and all that Uncle Henry could do to try to stop it was by his swaying vigorously in disgust and disbelief at the horror and, of course, the recent murder of Caroleena O'Ree, just days before, brought all the shocking memories of old together, reminding the tree that enough was enough. For all he knew, Uncle Henry was an old tree up in years, with not much life left in him. Uncle Henry was tired. And a little piece of him died that day.

Typically, live oak trees can live well over sixty years or more, sometimes, even to the grand old age of 250 to 500 years old. Through modern science and the study of trees—this is called dendrology—scientists have discovered a few older live oak trees: the Angel Tree living on Johns Island near Charleston, not so far from Uncle Henry, whose sturdy roots are moored here in Graham Village, and one tree thought to be at least two thousand years old, existing in Temecula, California, known as the Pechanga Great Oak, both coastal live oak trees. Surely there must be something extra good about sandy soil, warm, humid air, and hot climate, and the salty, brackish waters that God himself allows for these types of trees to live so long in. For this, Uncle Henry was pleased for God's favor of bringing him to life.

Uncle Henry had taken in too much. He had hidden Frederick Barber against his wishes, had watched the baby being murdered, Barnabas and Emma drowning during the hurricane, and Caroleena getting shot. The will to live was no longer in him. Uncle Henry decided then and there that it was time to let go and let nature take its course.

But what else would Uncle Henry have to endure before his death? Only time would tell. But one thing he was certain of, the clock was ticking, evil had been reestablished and set in place once again here on Oak Ridge Plantation, and there was absolutely nothing that he could do to stop any of it.

A TRIBUTE TO THE LOW COUNTRY

As a young child growing up in South Carolina's Low Country, memories now flood my mind like countless reels of film whirling endlessly, playing out the hours of my youthful life on the big screen in my mind. The live oak trees provided the stage and their low-lying limbs with dangling gray moss became friends, playmates, and refuge. Endless entertainment was given to me, my siblings, and our cousins as we roamed and played and spent out our days on this twenty-six-acre tract of land my Mama and Paw purchased in February 1947.

Years later, our family moved to North Carolina, but the Low Country was never too far out of sight for our travels often took us there, back home.

I never said goodbye because my heart remained there. The Low Country still flows through my veins. What a wonderful, magical place it is. The Low Country wasn't just an experience; it was my heart and my soul, and growing up there helped frame the beginnings of who I am today.

It is difficult to choose just one memory, one picture, and one experience from this beautiful area. We have taken a lot for granted throughout decades in life for not admiring the grand beauty and unimaginable scenes this land holds at every bend or around each curve. I would say that we are trying to make up for that now. *Black Mingo* is our tribute to her, the Low Country.

ABOUT THE CONTRIBUTORS

Ann Glasser Milligan is happy to have contributed to the writing of *Black Mingo*, a historical fiction set in the Low Country of South Carolina. Books have always been important to Ann. She has spent many satisfying hours all her life reading mostly fiction books, escaping into the drama, mystery, and family/interpersonal relationships that come alive on the pages.

Being from North Carolina and visiting grandparents, aunts, uncles, and cousins in this region of South Carolina has allowed Ann to experience the feel of sand between her toes at gorgeous beaches, ride the waves of the Atlantic, smell the marshy low-lying areas, and see the majestic oak trees covered in Spanish moss. All of this plus listening to and learning from stories of the history and geography of the area from relatives over the years has opened her eyes to the era of slavery and plantation life. This has all helped weave the magic of the Low Country into her being.

Ann has lived in the Midwest for forty-one years and is retired and living in Elon, North Carolina, with her husband. She worked outside the home as a medical transcriptionist for twenty-five years in hospitals and clinics, but her most important role was in her family as wife and mother of two grown children who currently reside in Illinois and Missouri. Traveling to visit her son and daughter and seeing different sights all over the land is also important to her in retirement. Of course, wherever she goes in the world, there will always be a book in her hand.

*****

Julie Glasser Harrison is a mother of two grown children. This empty nester has been blessed to have them and a grandson. A widow of sixteen years, Julie finds that her children along with her siblings keep her very busy. Julie currently resides in Chapel Hill, North Carolina, with her cat.

Julie has always enjoyed cooking, reading, and writing. Her "heaven on earth" are the beaches in the Low Country. These have always given her refuge for peace and tranquility.

Julie is a retired schoolteacher who has the ability to find love and talents in each one of the children she taught over the years. She always taught the basics, along with using their imagination to strive for more.

Julie grew up in a small southern town with two sisters and one brother. She has always been enchanted with the Low Country and was blessed to be able to spend a lot of time there. Julie loves nothing more than sitting on a beach while the small waves encircle her feet. She loves staring out at the multi-hued colors of the Atlantic Ocean and feeling nothing but pure contentment. The Low Country is a sanctuary of God's creation, and she revels in it.

ABOUT THE ARTIST

As far back as she can remember, Samantha Dormio has always had a love for wildlife and wild places and believes that all life on Earth is worthy of great celebration. After many years of gaining incredible experience in all different flavors of wildlife conservation work, in 2022 Samantha became a full-time wildlife artist. She primarily uses watercolor in a whimsical-realism style to project the magic of each of her subjects. She also donates 10% of all profits to various wildlife conservation charities. Samantha is honored to be able to create artwork that celebrates and advocates for those without a voice of their own.

Samantha currently resides near Tampa, Florida, an area buzzing with incredible wildlife. She lives with her fiancé and two rescued pets, her cat and snake. Outside of work, Samantha enjoys exploring new areas, going on long walks outside, reading, and spending time with family and friends. You can learn more about Samantha as well as find more of her work on her website: www.wildplanetcreations.com. You can also keep up with her latest work and news updates on her Instagram: @wildplanetcreations. The cover artwork was painted by Samantha Dormio.

ABOUT THE AUTHOR

Nell Glasser Smith is a new author to the stage of writing. To be a published author was one of her first "bucket list" items added to her living, breathing list of hopes and dreams to accomplish during her lifetime. And *Black Mingo* is bringing this hope, this dream, to life.

Nell started working on *Black Mingo* in early 2000, but with children to raise and a career of her own, the book was put on the shelf, so to speak, but was never too far out of sight.

After retiring, Nell poured herself into keeping her two grandchildren, Greyson and Elyse, and now with that season of life complete, she most recently picked the book back up, after deciding it was time to start writing again. The time was right to pick up the mantle of writing *Black Mingo* and to see where this journey would take her.

Nell includes in her writing many factual stories and family events because she feels that each of us should live on through the legacy of our life's stories—living on as a testament that our footprint here on earth was meaningful and will not be forgotten. Nell has a strong faith and counts it a privilege to use her writing talent to honor God while honoring her family's history.

Nell uses semicolons in lieu of dialogue as a place to pause, hoping to give the reader the flavor of being read to, of being told a story face-to-face with the author. Nell does not recall having ever read a book in story format like *Black Mingo*, with little to no dialogue. Nell believes you will be mesmerized to the point of not wanting to put *Black Mingo* down and eagerly anticipating possible sequel books: *Mingo Runs Red* and *Mingo Damned*. They are in the works, so stay tuned!

> Let the heavens rejoice, let the earth be glad;
> let the sea resound, and all that is in it. Let
> the fields be jubilant, and everything in them;
> let all the trees of the forest sing for joy.
>
> —Psalm 96:11–12 NIV

Printed in the USA
CPSIA information can be obtained
at www.ICGtesting.com
CBHW051331291124
18172CB00041B/993